MASTERS OF PLAY

HER MASTERS BOOK 3

INES JOHNSON

THOSE JOHNSON GIRLS

Edited by Kasi Alexander

CHAPTER ONE

oday's kink club is not what most people would think. Especially not if they watched the theatrical version of *Fifty Shades of Grey*. Sure, there would be all manner of sex furniture like a Saint Andrew's Cross parked somewhere at the center of the room like an angel topping a Christmas tree. Dotting the edges of the space would be a spanking bench, where any naughty grown, consenting adult could come sit on Santa Dom's lap. Of course, there would be a bed where birthday suits would be unwrapped. Stockings would be stuffed with all manner of sex toys, like dildos, butt plugs, nipple clamps, and spreader bars.

What would most likely not be found in this particular wonderland is Christian Grey himself.

Instead, a version of Old Saint Nick without the six-pack abs and full head of dark hair would deck these halls.

The vast majority of kinkster men weren't tall, dark, and twenty-something broody billionaires. They were mostly average height, thinning hairline, dad bod geeks and nerds. To the discerning eye that wouldn't take away from their attractiveness — unless a play partner was actually looking for a sadistic sugar daddy dressed in a red suit lined with fur. And, yes, there are some of those.

What made today's kinksters—men, women, and non-binary persons—truly attractive gifts that everyone on the naughty list couldn't wait to unwrap was that they knew exactly who they were, and they weren't afraid to say exactly what they wanted and needed to get off.

"Fuck, sir," moaned a woman walking along the floor of the kink club. Beside her walked a man dressed in leather pants and no shirt. Every few steps, he'd reach over and punch the woman in her arm.

"Fuck, sir," she moaned again after the latest punch. There was a hitch in her step, like she was trying to press her legs together to savor an orgasm while also putting one foot in front of the other to keep her stride.

Her play partner gripped her upper arm, right over the darkening red spot where he'd given her those love taps. The woman closed her eyes, and her steps faltered. But the man held her firm until she stopped her shivering and got her legs back under her. When she was steady enough to walk again, he switched to the other side.

"Fuck, sir," she cried again as he picked up the ritual on the other side and punched her in her other arm.

The ways in which kinksters got off was another misconception. It wasn't all about cuffs and collars. Hell, a soccer mom could pick up a pair of fur-lined cuffs and a dildo at the Walmart nowadays. What used to be kinky a few years ago was mainstream today. Take, for instance, the fact that in the 1950s, oral sex was considered kinky. Now college coeds have no problem asking for a backdoor entrance at the local kegger.

"Ah, fuck you, you fucking asshole."

That came from a man bent over a spanking bench. It wasn't Santa giving him a naughty whack on the ass. It was Mrs. Claus dressed in a red leather harness that held a purple dildo. Said dildo was being plunged enthusiastically into the man's asshole.

"Tell me how much you like it, you little bitch," said Mrs. Claus with another thrust that sent the man up onto the balls of his feet.

"Fuuuuck," was his response as his eyes closed and his whole body convulsed into shudders.

Kink was all about perception. I know because I've been studying it since the first time a boy slipped his fingers down my panties and rubbed me to orgasm. I've been chasing that bliss since high school... okay, middle school. I was promiscuous and I'm not ashamed. I strung up my kink flag early in life. Yeah, the cloth might be a little tattered from waving in some mighty storms.

"You here to study tonight, Kellie? Or you here to play?" asked the bartender.

"Both," I told him, taking the offered drink and downing it in one go. The amber liquid burned my throat and woke me up.

"You just let me know if you need a new test subject, honey."

"Thanks." I gave him a wink and the empty shot glass.

That part—the observation part—of my work was done. I didn't need any more participants in my study. All my data had been collected, all my findings collated, even the proofread of my dissertation was done.

Tomorrow, I would present the completed document to my dissertation chair. That would be a trial in and of itself. Tonight, I was going to celebrate.

I headed to the far reaches of the club. Past the Saint Andrew's Cross. Past the spanking benches. In a dark corner of the space was a simple, human-sized tripod with rope dangling from its arch. A shiver ran through my body, and I arched up on the balls of my feet with anticipation.

Like I said, kink has always been my subject of choice. I studied psychology in undergrad. I was a few days away from earning my PhD in Behavioral Health with a focus on gender, sex, and deviant behaviors. My area of expertise? Kink, of course.

Remember what I said about kink being a matter of perception? Well, the only way to know what kink was to others was to get into their bedroom. Surprisingly, most couples who are about to engage in sex aren't into letting a student into their boudoir to study their moves. Well, some are into that. But even those swingers don't like to be asked questions mid-fuckery. Though if you came into a BDSM club, you'd find many of the folks within the four walls are all too happy to let their kink flags fly and explain the meaning of each color on the flag as said flag was getting a rise.

What I discovered was that there are scales of kink. Most self-identifying kinksters were into the extreme side of the scale. For example, blindfolds were kinky. But being sensory deprived with a hood over your face and most of your body covered in latex was seriously kinky. Especially if you were also being led around on a leash while others present were allowed to finger and fondle you like that girl was having done to her at the center of the club.

Hickeys were pretty naughty. But being bruised on purpose, and then showing the patterns off like they were an accessory, was seriously kinky. Especially if you were particular about how you're being bruised. Like the guy in the corner getting off over knife play.

These days everybody and their mama was into spanking. Trust me, I know. Late one night as a kid, I woke from hearing a rhythmic thudding. Then I heard my mom call my dad *Daddy* and ask him to spank her harder. Kinky? Scarring? Not as scarring as watching the welts form on the woman's ass in the corner as her partner canes her with a stiff rod.

Me? I like to be tied up. Tight. And then

suspended. Just like that pixie of a girl who was dangling from ropes on the tripod. The two men working on her were adept as they tied the rope and lifted her higher. My mouth watered at the sight, impatient for her scene to end so that mine could begin.

CHAPTER TWO

Unfortunately, patience wasn't one of my virtues.

I worked hard not to tap my colorful Converse against the floor as I watched the redheaded girl in front of me finish up her turn. The blond-haired rigger worked the rope with dexterous fingers. Long, nimble fingers that I knew from experience were adept at making a bottom feel both secure and weightless as he tightened the ropes around the most intimate parts of their bodies.

The redhead wobbled as he unknotted the ropes that had made her fly. The blond grabbed hold of her right upper arm, but she was so off balance that she listed to the left. Luckily for her, a mirror image of the first blond man grabbed hold of her left forearm. She was sandwiched between the Carson twins, which was exactly where I was hoping to be by now.

"Take it easy, Ginger," said Owen Carson.

I could tell them apart easily. Mainly because Owen was the chatty one. Those twin dimples on either side of Owen's face were always on display because he was always grinning. Meanwhile, Alan kept his strong, square chin on display at all times.

"Make sure you hydrate," Alan scolded as he guided the teetering girl over to a couch. "Owen will see to your aftercare."

"What about you?" the redheaded Ginger pouted.

Amateur, I wanted to scoff. Alan Carson was only interested in binding and suspending women. He liked sweeping them off their feet. When their toes hit the ground again, he lost all interest.

"I've got you, Ginger," Owen said as he sat the girl down and began wrapping her up like a newborn.

Many bottoms and submissives enjoyed the secure feeling of a snug blanket after a scene. Especially if they weren't in a relationship with the Top or Dominant, who would cuddle with them later.

Alan Carson wasn't the cuddly type. Which was fine with me. My time working with other kinksters, helping them come to grips with their desires and erasing as much of the shame as possible —that was the scene that gave me satisfaction. It was when I was being bound and strung up by the Carsons that was my aftercare.

"Professor Prince, how goes the sexy research?" Owen asked after tucking the last fold of the blanket around Ginger.

Ginger glared at me as Owen straightened and held his hand out to me. Whatever. Her time was up.

Owen and Alan were Pro Doms—Dominants whose skills were for hire. The beauty of a Pro Dom was the ability to explore one's kink without the messy notions of a relationship or love or any kind of feelings. Owen didn't even have to exchange these pleasantries with me. It was just his personality.

His brother was the exact opposite. Alan simply wanted to get down to business. He watched our exchange from beneath a hooded gaze as he prepared the ropes for me.

"The research is done," I said to Owen as I watched Alan wrapping rope around his bare forearms.

"You're done?" Owen perked up. "Does that mean we can fuck you now?"

It was unethical for a researcher to dabble in her own research, if you know what I mean. But watching and recording all of this kink over the last few months while not fully participating had gotten me tied up in knots in the bad way. That's when I started employing the services of the Carson twins. But only for a little afterwork release.

I think that may have been what sparked the twin's extracurricular interests in me. The fact that I said I couldn't fuck them, let alone wanted to. I think it became a game with them. At least for Alan.

"I'm almost done," I said. "I just have to give my final presentation next week."

"So does this mean we can play doctor?" Owen waggled his eyebrows at me.

From her space on the couch, Ginger's scowl deepened. Her green eyes shot daggers at me. Luckily, there was nothing she could do physically, being wrapped up in a cocoon.

"Not yet," I said. "But I'll make another appointment with you next week when I technically am a doctor."

"In addition to your standing appointment?" said Owen. "Rewards mean extra."

"Yes," I said. "Put me down for two."

"You ready to fly, Kellie?" asked Alan, two sets of rope dangling from his hands.

"Yes, please," I said.

After all the hard work, it was time to celebrate. And by celebrate, I wanted to fly. I wanted to forget the last bits of data sets. I wanted to forget all the late nights in the library. I wanted to be free of all the snickers and jeers from my classmates.

No one took my research seriously. But then again, no one took the research of Masters and Johnson seriously. Now they had a television show done about them. No one took Graphenberg seriously, but today's woman thanked him every time someone hit their G-spot.

And I wasn't done.

I wanted to do more studies on the female orgasm. Why some women could achieve them so easily. Why they eluded others. I wanted to teach women that their orgasm didn't depend on men. It was theirs for the taking.

But that would be my next battle. Tonight, I just wanted to fly.

"What kind of knots would you like tonight, Kellie?" asked Owen as he took the small, pencil-thin dreadlocks of my hair and pulled them back into a single queue.

Another African American woman would've slapped a white man's hands if he dared to touch her hair. But Owen had asked permission the first time we played together. That permission had more to do with my safety than any fetish curiosity. It would be far too easy for one of my locks to get tangled up in the rope and cause me an injury.

"The tight kind," I said.

Owen's grin spread wider, showcasing his gleaming white incisors. He stepped closer, and his hot breath brushed my forehead. The goosebumps rose along my forearms. The hairs pricked up at the back of my thighs.

"Do you need to come?" Alan asked.

"God, yes."

He nodded, unwinding a length of rope from his hands as I pulled my T-shirt over my head and then shimmied my jean skirt down my hips.

Now I know I just said that an orgasm is a woman's responsibility, but damn if it didn't feel twice as good when she doesn't have to do all the work. I stood nearly nude, dressed only in a bra and panty set and my Converse. I had no issues with public nudity. The underwear thing was a rule from the Carsons. There was no penetration included with their services.

"You'll come," said Alan. "But only when I say you can."

"Sure," I snorted as I came to stand in front of the tripod.

"If you please me and behave, I'll let you come more than once. If you misbehave and don't follow my commands, all you get is the one."

I held out my hands, palms up, and bowed my head. But not before rolling my eyes. Alan saw it. I made sure he saw it. I wasn't a brat by nature, but he brought it out of me.

At the center of the three legs of the tripod hung a metal hoop. Alan placed a rug before the rig. "Come," he said. His voice was full of command and sent a shiver down my spine.

Owen picked up a length of rope and walked toward me. I stared at the rope, and my breath caught in my throat.

"Are you ready for us, Kellie?" asked Owen. Or at least, I think it was Owen. The only time I couldn't tell them apart was when they began tying me up with rope.

"Yes," I said.

My skin prickled as the air conditioning kicked on from above, blowing at the fine hairs on my forearms. My ears perked up, listening for any instructions. My eyes were so focused, I clearly saw the eyes staring at me from the back of the room. It was sensation overload.

"Hands."

My hands came up on their own accord and I presented the twins with my wrists.

"Good girl."

That was Alan. I knew because he loved to use my praise kink against me. With just those two words, my knees went weak. Suddenly, I wanted to please him. I wanted to be his teacher's pet.

Alan took my wrists in his hands. His touch was electric. He guided my hands behind my back, folding one forearm over the other. His chest pressed into my back as his hips and torso met my ass. His belt buckle brushed against the skin of my lower back.

He began to wrap the rope around my wrists. The feel of the ropes and their restriction ignited something within me. I was at his mercy, the mercy of his sure hands.

Owen rested his chin in the crook of my neck as he pulled the ropes taut. My head lolled back to rest against his cheek. I tilted my head up, offering him my lips. There was a part of my brain that knew he would never kiss me. But the highest part of the brain was not in control when the pleasure senses were ignited.

"Spread those pretty thighs."

That was Owen's voice. His voice was always soft, with a hint of humor. Owen stood in front of me, those dimples on display, as he grinned at me. I did as he bade me and widened my stance.

"Good girl," said Alan, pulling the binds on my arms tight.

And there it was again. That pleasing purr that moved like honey over my senses.

"Do not come," Alan commanded. "If you come now, it will be the only time I allow it. Do you understand?"

No, no I didn't. Well, actually I did. It was classic reverse psychology. But I was too smart for it.

At least I thought I was…

In front of me, Owen wrapped the rope around my waist, his thumb and forefinger brushing over my flesh. I was so hypersensitive that I sensed the difference in temperature of his fingernails as he threaded the ropes, and then the pads of his fingers as he pulled the rope taut against my skin. I couldn't understand how his hands were so dry when my palms were sweaty in anticipation.

Out before me, a sea of eyes stared at me. Heads

tilted to the side, teeth bit into lips, fingers brushed over chins or other body parts as I stood on display. Alan's touch made my nipples hard. Owen's breath against my abdomen made my pussy slick.

It was too much sensation. I had to shut my eyes. The loss of one of my senses did not de-tune me. Desire was a fume cloud in the air that invaded my lungs with every inhale.

And then there was the touch of the ropes. The thread they used was silky and coarse at the same time. It moved like satin on my skin as he made his loops. Then every time I made the slightest movement against the grain, I met with a delicious friction. I had to fight to keep still and not squirm for the sheer pleasure of it.

Owen ended the first bit of knot work with an intricate large node that rested on my belly button. The weight of it sparked desire in my belly, and that desire sank lower into my throbbing wet pussy. I was on fire and soaked at the same time.

Alan passed the ropes between my legs. I nearly buckled over as the dry rope hit my slick wetness. Alan kept me upright as he pulled the ropes up the crack of my ass like a G-string. With his fingers, he arranged the ropes at my pussy on either side of my clit.

"Do. Not. Come," he warned me.

I wasn't scoffing or rolling my eyes at him any longer. I was simply trying to keep what wits I had left in working order.

My lips were trembling at this point. There was a tremor in my hands as I tried to hold still as they continued. This was the sweetest agony I'd ever experienced in my life—and we were less than ten minutes into the scene. I gritted my teeth, balled my hands into fists, and tried to rein in the increasing pleasure.

Alan continued the knot work behind me until another heavy knot rested at the base of my spine. Each tug of his ropes brushed against the bind at my pussy. The ropes squeezed around my clitoris. My legs were shaking. When I began panting, Alan stopped. He came around front and stared at me. He didn't need to use his words to warn me not to come.

"I didn't," I said. "But I really, really want to."

Alan's hard veneer cracked a smile. "You're being a very good girl, Kellie. I'm very pleased with you."

The fucker. Why the hell did I ever tell him I had a praise kink? I wanted to preen under his compliments, and at the same time, I fucking wanted to come ignoring his edicts.

I felt an orgasm knocking on the door. I gritted my teeth and pressed my heels into the floor. Both twins stood and gazed down at me. Owen grinned, enjoying the fact that I was so close to pleasure. Alan, on the other hand, was enjoying the torment.

They waited a moment, watching me. Alan's expression told me he expected me to fail in this moment, to come against his command. Hell, I expected myself to fail.

But I didn't. I got a hold of myself before my muscles clenched. I raised my chin at him.

Alan smirked. I could tell he was surprised I hadn't failed.

Owen grinned brighter. I could tell he was impressed I had succeeded.

Alan reached the rope over my head and looped it on to the ring of the human-sized tripod. He gave the rope a tug, and I was airborne.

Finally!

The ropes took all of my weight and left me without a care in the world. They cradled me in the twine, leaving me with nothing to hold on to. There was nothing holding me back. I was restrained, but I was free. This was bliss.

Owen gave me a gentle shove, and I was truly flying. As the slight breeze hit me in the face, the ropes pressed against my pussy, giving me a rough friction. On the way back, I felt the pressure in my ass.

There was nothing I could do now. There was no floor to ground myself to. I clenched my hands, but it wasn't enough. An orgasm was coming soon, whether I wanted it to or not.

Next, Alan wrapped a chain around my breast. The cold metal was a shock to my system. It brought my attention from the heat between my thighs to my pussy and ass. My mind reeled between the cold chain, the friction of the rope, and the heat both materials created. And then there was Alan, whose hands continued to tug at the ropes and run against my skin.

Alan pulled out a magic wand vibrator. He placed the wand on the ropes. The vibrations went through the ropes and directly to my clit. My hips jerked, making the ropes seesaw against my front and back openings.

"You want it?" he asked.

"Yes."

"Beg me."

"Whaa?"

Alan turned the vibrator off and crossed his arms.

"Please, Alan, please let me come."

Alan turned the vibrator back on. Just the sound had me jumping out of my skin. In my peripheral vision, I saw people gathering closer to watch. I didn't care. Let them all see. I'd lick his shoes, the floor, anything for this orgasm.

"Please, sir. Please." It became a chant. "Please, please, please. Please, please, please."

Finally, he put the vibrator back on the ropes. My stomach fluttered. My panting diaphragm caused the ropes to rub against my skin. My heart pounded. I was breathless. I tingled all over.

Sparks flew like in a magician's spell. It was like my body was liquid and the vibrator was an electric cord. I lost control of my limbs as they jerked in each direction in response to my clenching inner muscles.

The orgasm started at my clit, but then traveled down the rope to my labia. As I clenched internally, the twine between my ass cheeks dinged pleasure sensors I'd never known existed, which then zipped back down to my labia and back up to my clit. The cycle repeated on a loop until I blacked out.

CHAPTER THREE

"There she is, Slut PhD."

The words were shouted out from a little grassy knoll on the side of the School of Psychology building on campus. The missive was hurled by Chad Hollinger. Yes, his name was actually Chad. Around said Chad, a few other coeds snickered at the insult. The thing they didn't get was that I was the one who came up with the nickname.

They certainly didn't know I'd coined the term months ago when I was with Chad. And when I say *with him,* I mean he was licking my boots, begging for a chance to get at my bare toes, all while calling me Dr. Slut. And groveling while wearing nothing but one of my lace thongs tight over the crack of his ass.

Chad was into degradation kink. And he had a mighty big foot fetish. He got hard when I put the heel of my boot right up against his testicles.

Again, I'm not judging anyone's kink. What I was judging was his reaction when I told him our play dates were done. I'd quickly gotten bored because I wasn't getting anything out of it. He wouldn't go down on me unless I left it messy down there. Like any self-respecting woman wouldn't take care of her hoo-ha just cause her dude liked to feel depraved.

"How goes your studies in ED, Chad?" I asked.

His face contorted. Chad was getting a doctorate in education. Yes, parents of America, this douche would soon be in a school near your little ones. All the smart graduate students, including Principal Chad, knew I wasn't referring to functional teaching methods. I was rather referring to a standing dysfunction.

"All my data points are fine," said Chad. "That's not what I hear about your entry points."

Whoa, that was a nice recovery. Totally unexpected of someone with his level of brain cells. But the douche was tussling with a master. Or rather, a mistress.

"I just came back from having my entry points double-checked, so I'm good to go, thank you."

A ruffle of unease and interest came around the group. I made a mental note to catalogue which coeds lifted a brow in curiosity. Only to quickly discard it.

I wasn't interested in playing with newbies any longer. From now on, I was keeping my dance card for the professionals. I would only be handing out professional business cards to old and new kinksters alike as a guide to sexual, emotional, and mental health.

I would've included Chad in that bunch. The man was clearly suffering from what we call subdrop. Subdrop happened when a sub, or in some cases even a Top, had trouble adjusting back to reality after coming out of a scene. It was an actual physical phenomenon because the drop in endorphins could cause fatigue, sadness, and actual aches and pains. It took some kinksters awhile to rebalance the endorphins and hormones in their body. If not addressed, subdrop could lead to depression.

The symptoms usually lasted a few hours, sometimes days. There had been a few extreme cases where the person was low for weeks. I'd cut Chad off months ago. I didn't think he was an extreme case. This was his normal temperament. He was, well, a Chad.

The truth was, no one was truly vanilla these days. Everyone had a kink. The only vanilla position left was missionary. Which always baffled me that that was the standard when human beings were clearly designed to do it doggie style. So weren't the deviants the ones who laid flat on their backs?

Anyway, I'd stopped listening to Chad's comebacks awhile ago. Having lost all interest in the back and forth, I took a step to walk away from Chad and his bunch of vanilla beans. That's when the fool grabbed my arm.

In a move that would've made my Taekwondo teacher proud, I twisted Chad's arm. The man dropped to a knee. I immediately let him go when he looked up at me from beneath a gaze hooded with desire clear in his eyes.

Exactly who was the slut here?

"Hey," he whispered low enough for only me to hear. "I am available if you need another test subject for your research."

"Did you know that fifty percent of women are into rape fantasy?" I asked him, my gaze still on that hand that had so offended me. I took a deep breath like I'd learned in martial arts class and tried to remember that I wasn't supposed to use the art for ill will.

"What?" said Chad.

I'd clearly caught him off guard. There was a spark in his eye, a spark of interest.

"These women don't want to be raped," I continued my explanation. "They want consensual non consent."

The haze in his gaze grew. The desire was clearly growing. If I brushed up against him, I knew he would be hard. Ew.

"Surprisingly, the same percent of men want to be forced to have sex as well. The only thing I've never been able to figure out about you is if you want to dip your stick into a honey pot, or if you want a stick dipped into your—"

"Bitch!" he hissed. But he was smarter than I thought. He only used his words this time.

"I wasn't shaming you, buddy," I said. "That's your shame talking. I'll send you a copy of my dissertation once it's published."

Students gave me a wide berth. A few looked up at me with curiosity. A few with open desire. But I wasn't here to play today. I was here to work.

Once my dissertation was defended, meaning approved by the board, then I could get on with my life. I wouldn't have to answer to these people anymore. I wouldn't have to answer to anyone. I would be free to start my sexual health clinic. A place where even a Chad could come and work through his issues with shame and inadequacies.

My Converse squeaked as they moved from pavement to tiled floors. I'd spent far too many hours in this building. My blood, sweat, and tears were on the floor, under the desks, and all over the walls. But I was at the end. In fact, I could see the end.

At the end of the hall was the last hurdle I had to jump through to be free. Chad might've thought I was a hard ass. But he was still in his first year of graduate school. He hadn't yet had to stare into the face of the devil and not blink. I'd been doing that for the last two years.

I had no delusions that I was about to get my angel's wings. I at least hoped I'd leave this place with my soul intact. That was all up to the man behind the closed door. I just had to gird my loins before going in there. Luckily, my loins were still warm and toasty from the twins last night.

The door opened, and the sounds of crying preceded the person coming out. I had seen grown men sniffling uncontrollably as they walked out that door. This time it wasn't a grown man coming out. It was a woman. A redhead that I recognized.

Ginger stormed out of Professor Chase Sinead's office, her cheeks as flushed as her red hair. She was fully clothed, but a button on her blouse was askew.

A tall man darkened the doorway at her retreat. His brown gaze was hard, his chiseled chin high and set in its perpetual grimace. His black hair was swept back with a single gray streak just off center.

Professor Sinead, or rather Professor Sin, as many of his students called him, was only in his early thirties. That streak, we all knew, had come from his deal with the devil. No man should walk this earth with those looks and that amount of genius. He'd definitely made a deal with Lucifer.

It looked like Ginger had tried to make a deal with him and lost. Because Professor Sin was immovable when it came to feminine wiles. He was the same with masculine wiles, too.

To him, it all came down to what was in your brain, not below the belt. If you didn't have the right stuff, he would rake you over the coals. In the two years that he'd been my teacher and the chairman of my dissertation committee, he'd never once made me cry. My balls were too big for that.

"Ms. Prince."

My shoulders jerked back at the sound of that deep baritone that promised sin but would never deliver. Professor Sinead stood in the door like a dark prince. He beckoned me into the door, and I took a step into the bowels of hell. I wasn't worried about my soul. It was my dissertation that needed to come out intact, and I was well prepared for that.

CHAPTER FOUR

I'd been in this office several times over the years. It felt much like the principal's office back in high school. Though there were no motivational posters on the walls.

Professor Sinead's walls were bare, save for an academic calendar that was covered in black and red marker. Meetings and class schedules were in a sedate dark color while deadlines, testing dates, and end of period were carved in like what looked like blood. There was a little drip that brought to mind blood splatter hanging off the D of *semester's end.*

Shelving units and filing cabinets lined up like soldiers against every wall. On the flat tops of those were neatly stacked papers or books. Every edge of paper was aligned. Each book's spine perfectly straight. Nothing, not student, not parchment, would dare stray from the box Professor Sinead placed them in.

His organization system was clear. The As started in one corner. If my eyes followed the shelving around, I ended at the Zs. I bet if he dropped dead, anyone could come in here and take over his work.

No, that couldn't be true. No one could fill that man's six foot two form or size twelve shoes. Luckily, he wasn't in danger of dropping dead any time soon.

Professor Sin stood behind his desk, tall and erect. A study in lean lines of tense muscle. He never looked relaxed. He always reminded me of a coiled cobra, ready to strike at any second.

"Leave the door open," he said in his deep baritone. His voice had always vibrated through my ears and arrowed straight for my core.

I wasn't so special. His voice did that to every woman in his class. Anyone walking down the hall could look in and see every female's legs crossed under her desk as she leaned forward with baited breath, listening to Professor Sin's lectures of data sets and statistical analysis.

I gave the doorknob a little push. The frame

bounced quietly against the wall, opening wider than before. Down the hall, another door pulled shut. But not before I saw Dr. Wroth's silver and gold bun duck inside.

I'd actually never gotten a good look at the reclusive woman in all my years here. She didn't teach any classes at the university. The word was that her research was funded by the government, which kept the university, and the psychology department in particular, swimming in grant money.

"I've reviewed your methodology section in your dissertation, Ms. Prince."

I turned my attention back to the deep end I was currently swimming in. The devil in a dark suit thumbed over the document. As each leaf of paper left the flesh of his thumb and fell back in line, I felt he was thumbing through the contents of my soul… or my clit. I often wondered if the two were mutually exclusive.

"And you found it exemplary," I said.

Professor Sinead glanced up at me from beneath those lenses. I had a suspicion he didn't need the glasses. I was certain he only wore them to intimidate. I'd once caught him reading without them.

"It appears you're using only qualitative methods

in your study," he said, pushing a wayward sheet of paper back in alignment.

"That's correct."

"You can't believe that will be enough to form a robust study." Professor Sinead stood the stack of papers up lengthwise. The edges of the two hundred pages of my dissertation made a clacking sound as they met the top of the desk.

"I'm using several qualitative methods," I said. "I've used the phenomenological method to chronicle the lived experiences of my subjects. Then there's the ethnographic methodology employed as I prove that the BDSM culture is a subgroup. And finally, there's a case study where I perform an in-depth, descriptive investigation of the confined BDSM club where all the kinkery goes down."

Professor Sinead laid my dissertation down flat on his desk. Not a single one of the papers made a peep. When he shifted in his seat, there was an audible squeak of fine, firm ass against aged leather.

I perked up at the subtle squeak of the leather in his chair. Was I making him uncomfortable? Or was I making him aroused? Either was a win for me.

From the open door of his office, I heard raised voices. A student was arguing with a teacher. Likely, Dr. Santos was on the other end of that argument.

The man was a hard-ass when it came to citations. He once failed a student because two entries in his bibliography were out of alphabetical order.

"As you know," I said, tuning out the argument on the other side of the wall, "my study looks at how those in the BDSM lifestyle label themselves and how kink is becoming more normalized in main society."

"To do that, you'll need numerical data sets."

"I disagree," I said. "Sir."

Professor Sinead's nostrils flared at that. I'd long suspected that the man was a Dominant. Not just because of how he ran a tight ship in his classroom, or the unbending organization of his office. It was because he could raise a single eyebrow in disdain. I'm certain that is a skill that only Dominants are born with.

Sure enough, that right eyebrow rose as he stared down at me. The left one stayed put as though it couldn't be bothered to deal with my antics at the moment. I was usually a very assertive woman. This was the only man I'd ever brat it up for.

In true brat form, I gave him lip while also showing respect. I'd learned that trick in his statistical analysis class two years ago. I could momentarily trip him up if I disagreed with him but also called him sir. His eyes would flash at mine. His nostrils would flare. And that brow would go up.

"You think I'm doing this to punish you?" he said.

I wish. I almost said that out loud. Damn, if I didn't want those large hands to spank my ass, or pull my hair—right at that spot, right at the nape of my neck. The place where big cats grab up their young. Oh, I wanted this lion of a man to grab me by my scruff and give me a shake.

"It's not just me you have to impress, Ms. Prince."

"Have I ever impressed you. Sir?"

That brow crept up higher, but Professor Sin ignored my question. "Dr. Worth and Dr. Santos will be at your dissertation defense. They will pick apart your findings without a quantitative data set."

"My research doesn't need it. I've proven my thesis without it."

"With oral data only."

"Oral is the best kind of data." I sat back in the chair and crossed my arms. "Sir."

Professor Sinead's nostrils flared. His hands balled. He leaned forward.

My legs were already crossed. I squeezed my ass down in the chair, certain I was leaving a wet spot. I didn't care. I needed the friction, if only to keep myself from hopping across the damn desk and humping his leg.

My multiple orgasms at the rope of the twins last night were a thing of the distant past. In front of Professor Sinead, I always felt like a virgin willing to throw herself at the dragon to be sacrificed. Damn, I bet he'd make roasting in a fire feel so good.

Professor Sinead took a deep breath through those flared nostrils. He lowered his right brow to meet with his left. Finally, he leaned back in his seat, a squeak announcing his retreat.

I leaned back too, but there was no squeak at my movement. The seat was too wet. I'd need a white flag to mop up the mess I'd made.

"I'm trying to help you, Ms. Prince."

"You're trying to make me over in your own light," I insisted. "Or rather, in your own digits. You don't respect qualitative data."

"I'll admit I have a bias. If you'll admit you have a weakness."

I sat up straighter. Forget the white flags, that was a red flag being thrown. A foul on the play. "What weakness?"

"The only time you got a B during your studies here was in my quantitative statistics class."

"I deserved that point to bring me from an 89 to a 90, and you know it."

The corner of Professor Sinead's mouth quirked. It wasn't a smile. He never smiled. I knew from two years of studying his minute facial expressions that this was his amused look.

"You took shortcuts in the data sets of your final exam, Ms. Prince."

"I'm not now. There is no place for numerical data in my study. This is all about people and their experiences and feelings. You can't take sexual experiences and boil them down to ones and zeroes. It's far too nuanced."

We'd had this argument for the last year when I'd announced the topic of my research study. Professor Sinead had argued that I had to add numbers to my data points. One thing he never did was ridicule my thesis that centered on sexual kinkery.

"If you don't believe me, come see for yourself."

The words were out in the air between us before I could take them back. Luckily, I knew he would never—

"Fine," he said. "I will."

CHAPTER FIVE

"You invited your professor to come to a sex club?" asked Maree.

"I didn't invite him... exactly."

"But he's coming here?" said Josie. "Professor Sin is coming here? Tonight?"

I took a deep inhale instead of answering her. Then I held my breath. I wondered if I held it for long if it could make him not show up. When the breath burst out of me in a sudden whoosh, I wondered if I in fact did want him to show up.

Professor Sinead had been the only teacher to ever give me anything other than an A. He had been the only teacher in my life that hadn't offered me constant praise. The man was impossible to impress.

He was also wrong about my data. I had taken

meticulous notes. I knew that my dissertation was solid and would pass muster. There was a big part of me that wanted to show him that and prove him wrong. And then finally, he'd look at me and say, *Well done, Ms. Prince.*

Just the thought of those two words—*well done*—and I was squirming on the barstool. Luckily, there were white clothes a plenty in the club to wipe up the messes that members left behind. Because the thought of any positive affirmation coming from those perpetually frowning lips was a wet dream for me. Like I said, in addition to my bondage and suspension fetish, I had a praise kink.

"Look at her, Mo," said Josie. "Our girl is all hot and bothered. She's hot for teacher."

"Oh, I wanted a good show tonight, and now I'm gonna get one," said Maree.

"I'm just going to show him around. He'll probably clutch his tie and barely cross the threshold."

But somehow I doubted that. The looks on my friends' faces said they doubted it too. Maree rubbed her hands together, as though warming them up in front of a fire on a cold evening. Josie pressed the back of her hand to her head in a faux fainting gesture. I was so used to being the one joking and poking fun at their love lives. For the first time, I was in the hot seat, and it was not the least bit comfortable.

"Pervert," I said to my two besties. "This is my lab."

I opened my arms to encompass the club. The doors had opened under an hour ago, and already things were in full swing. And by full swing, I mean there were men and women hanging from sex swings performing all manner of acrobatic sex. It was the Queen's birthday, and this was how she chose to celebrate.

The Queen had been a fixture in this place long before I'd gained my membership card. She mostly liked to be carried around on a throne by two muscular men. Her throne, as well as her ballgown, was ass-less. She was paraded around her subjects—which encompassed everyone in the club—with her ass on display. If she found a subject worthy, they could come and kneel down.

Not before her.

Beneath her.

With specter in hand, the Queen dubbed one lucky subject worthy. The man knelt down as the Queen's two muscular guards held her aloft. The prostrate man now had direct access to the Queen's family jewels where he could worship at her leisure.

The Queen's head lolled back. Her white pompadour of a wig went slightly askew as she trembled from the pleasure of being worshiped. I was momentarily distracted watching the scene play out.

I wasn't the only one. Maree and Josie and I all sipped at our glasses as we watched the boss bitch get her due.

"Now that's what I call a retirement plan," said Maree.

The Queen was easily over fifty. No amount of makeup could hide the wrinkles surrounding her gray eyes. Even with the mask she wore, she couldn't hide those crow's feet. And what woman would care if she could still command that kind of devotion at any age?

"I wonder if she gets dental with that," said Josie.

"That certainly looks like an oral exam to me," I said.

The three of us threw our heads back in a fit of giggles. This was my idea of a retirement plan. Girls' night out with my two best friends in the world. Whether it be at a sex club, or cocktails on the beach, or even mimosas at the retirement home. All I needed was my friends by my side.

"Oh, Master Cornelius is here," said Josie,

downing her drink and hopping off the bar stool. "Duke made him a new flogger. Well, he made it for me, but he gave it to Master Cornelius to use on me. He promised the material he used would give a real good sting."

And with that, Josie weaved her way through the crowd to greet her three boyfriends. Master Cornelius, the artist who looked more like a pirate than a painter, scooped her up and bent her backwards for a kiss. When he righted her, Josie's old Dom Duke and former stalker pressed a kiss to her forward, while also wrapping a possessive arm around her waist. Josie leaned into Duke as she turned her head to take yet another kiss from her business partner, Frank Gunn.

She was surrounded by a sea of bliss. And I was happy for her. Though I had to amend my fantasy to include those three guys and—

"Oops, I'm gonna be late for my own date," said Maree, putting down a few bills to cover all our drinks. "If I miss you before you leave, call me in the morning to tell me everything."

Maree bussed a kiss to my cheek before hurrying off in the other direction. A door opened just down the hall, and Maree was yanked inside. I couldn't tell which of her three lovers tugged her inside, but I knew all three of them were there. Paul Brooks, the billionaire businessman who was also Maree's boss. Kaiden Louis, Paul's silent business partner and former playboy, who now performed and played only with Maree. And the quietly intense toy maker Sam Kringle who engineered sex toys that he would test on Maree before putting them on the market for other women to enjoy.

I sat alone on the barstool, running my finger around the half empty shot glass. I'd never been interested in having a long-term monogamous relationship myself. I'd known from an early age that I wanted to be married to my work. I doubted any man would stand to play second to his wife's work as a sex therapist.

Turning to the sound of pleasure, I saw the Carson twins at work. They were binding a petite girl. That same redheaded Ginger that they'd played with last time. Her eyes were closed in the ecstasy that came with feeling the fibers tighten on flesh. When they opened, they locked first on Alan.

Alan gave her an assessing glance. Cool and professional, as always. He was interested in her pleasure, but only at the touch of the rope. He made sure to avoid too much flesh-to-flesh direct contact.

That was his way of not letting his bottoms become attached.

I could've told him the tactic wasn't foolproof. The chemicals that flooded the body during sexual pleasure were hard to distinguish from emotional love. It was far too easy to confuse them, whether on a drunken one-night stand or soberly negotiated play.

Ginger was in a world of her own as she reached for Alan. The man deftly caught her hands and bound them tight, easily avoiding her touch. Ginger's features were at first a pout, but then her eyes skated past me and turned to alarm. The expression on her face looked as though she'd seen the devil himself walk into the club.

Because the devil had arrived.

Professor Sinead was standing just behind me. That shrewd gaze was not on the naked, writhing bodies on the floor. They were not on the Queen, who was frantically motioning her throne to be set down. They were not on Ginger, who was now struggling in her ropes. He was staring straight at me.

"Ms. Prince."

"Professor Sin."

He quirked an eyebrow.

"Sinead," I corrected. "Professor Sinead, you're here."

"As I said I would be." He reached up to straighten his tie. He didn't tug to loosen it. He looked entirely at ease in this den of iniquity.

A tingle went up my spine as I wondered if I'd been right all along. Was Professor Sinead so at ease here because he was a Dom?

"Shall we begin, Ms. Prince?"

CHAPTER SIX

"Of course I begin my dissertation with a history of the practices of kink." My steps were slow as I led Professor Sinead around the club. I'd tried to speed up our progress, thinking the man would indeed be clutching his pearls, or rather his silk tie, at the displays on the floor. But nope.

Professor Sinead was completely unfazed by the *Fuck You, Sir* couple. The bruises on the woman's arm were Fuji apple red as we walked by. The man's gaze down upon her was hungry, while her gaze up at him was completely adoring as they displayed their love language for all the world to see.

"What most people don't understand about the BDSM culture is that it's not always about sex," I continued. "In fact, it's often not about sex at all. It's about power, pain, and pleasure."

"Clearly," said Professor Sinead.

His gaze shifted from the couple and landed on the Queen. The older woman sat upon her chair, lifted in the air. Clearly visible beneath the hoisted chair were two half nude bodies, one with breasts, the other with a fully erect penis. Their faces weren't visible as they were buried beneath the Queen's dress.

For her part, the Queen's head was lolled back, eyes closed in ecstasy. A few of the feathers that dotted her silver wig floated around her shoulders and down to the floor as she writhed in ecstasy. She opened her eyes and caught my gaze. I could see the haze of pleasure clearing from her eyes in real time.

Her body went stiff as a rod, and she sat up, closing her legs. Beneath the chair, those pleasuring her gave a startled yelp. The chair teetered as the weight distributed and caught those carrying her off guard. It took a few moments to right the chair. Luckily, disaster was averted, so I continued on with my presentation to Professor Sinead.

"In ancient Mesopotamia, there are stories and depictions of the goddess Inanna where she would whip her subjects until they became aroused," I said, needing to fill Professor Sinead's silent observation with something. "The same images and stories of flagellation can be found in Greek art."

As if conjured up by my words, I saw Josie bent over a post. She was stripped down to her black and white underwear. I wanted to scowl at my friend for having such unimaginative lingerie when I noted that the black sketching on the white backdrop was a series of ones and zeros. My nerdy friend had clearly worn that for her equally nerdy computer whiz of a boyfriend, Frank Gunn.

Usually, Josie and her guys played in a private room. But I supposed they were displaying her boyfriend Duke's new creation. The flogger was a work of art. And, I noted, the black and white designe perfectly matched Josie's scant costume.

I wanted to applaud her monochrome-coordination, but I knew she wouldn't hear any praise other than Master Cornelius'. With a flick of his wrist, he sent the tails dancing across Josie's ass. She went up on her toes, and the rest of the world was lost to her.

When I caught Professor Sinead eyeing my friend with a raised eyebrow, I knew I was jealous. I just wasn't sure if the jealousy stemmed from an academic or emotional source. I was the one explaining the facts about whipping, yet he was watching Josie perform it.

I stepped in front of his gaze, blocking his view of my best friend's increasingly red ass. "And of course there's the *Kama Sutra*, which was one of the earliest instructive works on sex. There's a whole passage in there noting the six appropriate places to strike one's lover to elicit passion."

Professor Sinead blinked, his eyes slowly focusing on me. That single brow came down to join the other. Instinctively, my shoulders went back and my chin dipped. I did not submit easily, but something about this man made my knees go weak.

As though he sensed my submission, Professor Sinead nodded. He waved his hand like he was a Victorian gentleman and I was a lady in his care. I knew he wanted me to precede him, but the brat in me itched to defy him.

"And then there's courtly love," I said, "which was the most submissive of all."

That caught his attention. He cocked his head to the side in that way that said *prove it* without actually saying a word.

"Oh, come on," I said. "A manly knight who takes a vow of chastity and promises to take on any feat for his lady, including extreme pain, to win her.

Even though he would likely never have her because she was upper class and likely already engaged or married to the lord of the land. She was an object of his affection that he would never possess. It's the ultimate Master and submissive relationship, or rather Mistress and submissive relationship."

"Hmmm" was Professor Sinead's only comment.

I wanted to stomp my foot in irritation. Here I'd brought this buttoned-up scholar to a sex dungeon, and he was completely unruffled. He wasn't impressed with my dissertation. He wasn't aroused by my subject matter. I'd gone after both his heads, and he was completely unfazed. What did I have to do to get a rise out of him?

"We all know the history of the Marquis de Sade and sadism," I went on, just spewing random facts in a clear effort to prove my intellect. "And there's Leopold Von Sacher-Masoch and his stories of spanking and how pain was akin to joy, which led to the idea of masochism. Then came the 1950s' leather craze in biker culture, which gave us kinksters, our most popular fashion statement. And finally we land here in the present of the Internet age that has allowed us all to find ourselves and come out of the closet."

"Hmmm."

"Hmmm?" I stopped walking and rounded on him. "Is that all you have to say?"

"Your directive was to prove to me that you do not need a quantitative analysis as part of your study."

Oh, I'd forgotten about that bit. "Because I worked solely with observation and lived experiences, the stories told by the people in this club who are self-identified as kinksters."

"You employed a scale to rank their level of... kink."

I had to pause a moment and commit to memory the intonation of Professor Chase Sinead saying the word kink. It reminded me of the sound a key makes when it fits into a lock and turns.

"Yes," I said, "that's right. My extreme meter is calibrated on these members."

"Your extreme meter is a metric, Ms. Prince," said Professor Sinead. "A metric needs quantitative support."

"The extreme meter is the *result* of my study. I can't use the result in my data collection."

"You will if you want to prove that the meter works."

"It does work."

"How can you prove it?" Professor Sinead raised that eyebrow at me in challenge.

"It's based on an individual's perception of their own sexual deviancy. For example, mine."

As soon as the words were out of my mouth, I wanted to swallow them back down. Except I also wanted Professor Sin to see that I was right.

"Have you come to play, Kellie?"

I looked up to find Owen grinning down at me. Alan was behind him, winding rope around his forearm. Meanwhile, Professor Sinead stood at my back with his brow cocked and loaded. It was sensation overload.

"Yes," I said. "Yes, I have. But can we have a private room?"

CHAPTER SEVEN

"Who's this?" asked Alan.

"This..." I thought about lying for a split second. The problem was that I've never been good at it. The truth has always been my friend. Mainly because it was easier to remember since it's what actually happened in real life. "This is my teacher. He's here to check my work for my study."

"Hmm." Alan's tone sounded exactly like Professor Sinead's.

The two men were physically as different as could be. Alan had to be at least ten years younger than Professor Sinead, if not more. That wasn't to say that Professor Sinead looked aged. Not at all. But there was a maturity set in the smooth lines of his jawline. Whereas the arrogance of youth was what rounded out Alan's chin.

Professor Sinead also had a couple of inches on the twins. But all three men were lean and muscled. Not muscled in the bulky sense. They each looked as though they'd lettered on the swim or varsity team where their muscles were used in calculated movements and not for brute strength.

The starkest difference between the men was their coloring. The Carson twins were blessed with golden looks that the Greek gods would've envied. Golden locks of hair and golden tan skin. Meanwhile, Professor Sinead had been adorned with dark looks that I still believed came from Lucifer himself. Thick, dark waves crowned his head. His skin was more burnished tan than golden. He was only just a few shades lighter than my brown skin.

"Your teacher?" said Owen. "Does that mean this is a test?"

"Sort of," I said.

"And once you pass, we'll finally be able to fuck you?" said Owen.

"Hmm." Professor Sinead looked over at me.

"I haven't—" I started and stopped. "I didn't—"

"She said we couldn't have penetrative sex with

her until she was done with her study," said Owen, ever helpful. "Because it would be unethical."

"She was right about that," said Professor Sinead.

Professor Sinead looked around the room, taking in all the toys on the wall. An assortment of dildos, butt plugs, and vibrators lined one side. Floggers and canes lined another. Cleaning products were shelved on the third wall. There was no bed in this room. Just a tripod for suspension.

I cleared my throat, readying my analytical mind. I needed to explain this academically so that Sinead would understand. But it was hard to ignore the wetness gathering between my legs.

"I've identified as kinky since I was a teenager," I said as I began my impromptu presentation. "I've always liked when my partners held me down during sex. Being rough and using force is common in many bedrooms on this earth. Some people derive pleasure from it. Others don't. I later learned that my kink went beyond that, to an extreme."

I don't know what I expected Professor Sinead to do. He stared at me, expressionless. Both brows down. No tug at either corner of his mouth. He simply regarded me, waiting patiently. So I continued, while also unbuttoning my jeans.

"I derive the greatest pleasure not only from being held down and tied up. I experience the most amount of pleasure when I'm also suspended off the ground."

Professor Sinead blinked at me. That was the only sign that he was listening. Also, his blinking eyes didn't dip to my chest as I tugged my shirt over my head. I stood before my teacher in a matching bra and panty set—unicorn rainbow, of course. And like a courtly gentleman, he kept his gaze on my face, listening to my every word.

"That puts my perceived sexual deviancy near to the top of the meter, but I haven't hit a cap yet. Not on the high end and not on the low end. You're asking me to measure a scale that I'm in the process of building. That's not possible."

Now technically, I could've stopped this little demonstration there. I'd said my piece, and that was all I needed to say. But as Professor Sinead stood there looking me dead in the eye, I couldn't help myself.

My shoulders went back. My chin dipped. My hands went out, palms up, in an offering.

Professor Sinead did not take my offering. Alan stepped in front of him and took me in his hold. Behind Alan, Professor Sinead took a seat in the single wooden chair in the room. His gaze focused on me. I couldn't take my eyes off him.

"You're going to be a good girl, aren't you, Kellie?"

I had to think about Alan's question for a moment. I was not being a good girl at the moment. I was standing near nude in front of my teacher while two other men tied me up in an effort to show my level of kinkery.

Nope, this definitely wasn't good girl behavior.

Alan grinned at me as though he had graded my performance and came up with the same marking. He slipped the rope around my wrists and looped it into a knot. A tight knot.

"Do you need to come?" Alan asked.

It took everything inside of me to keep my gaze focused on Alan and not let it slide to Professor Sinead. It would not be a good look to come while he was watching me. But I doubted I'd have any control over that when the moment came. And I knew, with the gleam Alan had in his eyes, that he would make that moment come.

"You'll come," he said. "But only when I say you can."

I didn't even have it in me to offer a bratty comeback. I was truly fucked. Or at least I was about to be.

There was silence in the room for a few moments. All that could be heard was the whisper of rope as Alan and Owen worked their loops. The scritch of fibers as the boys tied their knots. And the squeak of shoes on tile as they moved around me in their efforts to get me bound and airborne.

There was dead silence from the corner of the room where Professor Sinead sat. I know because I didn't take my eyes off him the entire time I was being bound by the Carson twins. At times, it looked like Professor Sinead was barely breathing. More times than not, I know I was holding my breath.

With every touch of the rope tugging at my flesh, my breath caught. Every time my breath caught, Professor Sinead's nostrils would flare. His fingers would jerk. But other than that, he didn't move.

Alan slid a length of rope between my legs. He let the heavy twine rest in the nook of my thigh over the elastic of my panties. His gaze connected with mine, asking for permission he knew he already had. Though I was getting off having my professor watch me, I knew that Alan was the one truly in charge of my pleasure. He dangled the rope in my face.

"Please," I whispered.

"So eager tonight."

Alan rubbed the rope up my thigh. I closed my eyes and shivered. The rope was nowhere near my core. I didn't need it to be. I was bound, weightless, flying high. He could blow on me and I'd come.

"How's she doing, Professor?" asked Owen. "She gonna pass her class?"

"If she can quantitatively describe this experience, then yes."

My eyes flew open. "What?"

Alan chose that moment to swipe the rope over my clit. "Come for me, Kellie."

The orgasm slammed into me. My mind went into a haze as pleasure coursed through my core. My vision filled with Professor Sinead's face. My ears synched to the sound of his voice.

"This experience surpasses what I've read in your findings," said his deep baritone of a voice.

The tone was like honey, slipping and sliding over my body and making the orgasm linger. But the actual words scratched at something in my brain.

"The data needs to be both qualified and quantified to withstand the rigor it will be brought under by your dissertation committee. Frequency analysis should be employed here."

I was struggling. I was bound by the ropes into immobility, which is what I love. The hum of Alan's command to come was still sparking on my finger-tips and in my core with the aftershocks of my orgasm. But Professor Sinead's words were growing louder and louder in my head, like a storm picking up speed and ferocity.

Because he was right. He was fucking right. I should've employed frequency analysis to show that my findings were solid. And I hadn't.

I was no longer thinking of the fact that I'd just nutted in front of a man I wanted to impress intel-lectually. I was gutted that he'd found a flaw in my carefully crafted masterpiece. Shame stole the last vestiges of pleasure from me.

When I opened my eyes, the chair Professor Sinead had been sitting in was empty.

CHAPTER EIGHT

I don't remember falling asleep. I rarely do after a scene. I usually hightail it out of there after the last knot is untied. The intense feelings that came with a scene could lower inhibitions. For a lot of people, it was a stronger high than any manmade drug. The natural chemicals of endorphins, adrenaline and oxytocin were at sky high levels in the body, making subs and Doms alike feel like they were card-carrying members of the Justice League.

But after a time, that cocktail of natural chemicals would drop and the crash could wreak havoc not only on the body, but even more intensely on the mind. There were many a sub that would chase that particular high and make questionable decisions to get back to it, agreeing to scenes that could leave permanent physical or mental damage.

It was in that space of sub drop that I didn't care to be around others. I preferred to regain my equilibrium in private, or with my girls. Something about the Carson boys had always made me feel comfortable enough to rest in their care after they made me fly.

When I opened my eyes, I was wrapped up in something soft and warm. Well, mostly soft. More warm than anything. There were some hard planes there. And the planes smelled good. Like pine and chocolate and man.

I lifted one eyelid halfway to see that I was in fact wrapped up in a man. I was lying in Owen's lap. One of his muscled arms cradled my head. The other rested over my abdomen.

There was a phone in his hand. The colorful flashing lights caught my eyes. He was playing Candy Crush.

I was momentarily distracted by the game. The simplicity of it—matching three colored sweets in a row to achieve higher and then higher levels. It was satisfying to watch the reds and blues and yellow get placed together and disappear. But that's the draw of the game.

"Score!" said Owen as he squeezed the phone in one hand and my shoulder with his other hand. "I achieved the next level."

I shifted my body to look up into his eyes.

"You looked worried," he said, gazing down at me. "I always have a plan."

"It's not your plan. It's theirs. The makers of that game are using a tactic called a variable ratio schedule of reinforcement to engage the dopamine centers of your brain. They get you addicted to winning in the beginning, but it gets increasingly harder as you go on. It's the same tactic used to keep people at slot machines."

Owen put his phone down and picked up one of the locks of my hair. "Is that so?"

I was distracted watching him loop my hair around his index finger. He twined it tightly. So tightly that it drained the red from the tip of his finger.

"That's an interesting theory, Dr. Prince." Owen leaned in close until his lips touched the cone of my ear, making me shiver. "I think there's a little red cherry somewhere between your legs. Wanna see how many times I can tap it before it explodes?"

I giggled. I actually fucking giggled.

Owen had always been so easy to be around, so

easy to let my guard down in front of. He was the one who always gave me exactly what I wanted in a scene without making me wait or beg for it.

Right now, he was letting my hair unravel from his fingertip. That finger traced down my forearm. The coldness from loss of blood left the tip as it trailed down my warm flesh, heading farther and farther south.

"Don't you have more sessions?" I asked.

"You were our last one. You usually are."

"I am?"

Owen nodded as his finger slipped beneath the blanket he'd wrapped me up in. "Because of the aftercare."

"I didn't ask for aftercare. You don't have to—"

"Not your aftercare. Mine."

His arms didn't tighten around me. In fact, he relaxed. Owen slouched down into the back of the couch, allowing my body to slip farther between his open legs and allowing space to farther part my thighs.

"I'm your aftercare?" I asked.

Again, Owen nodded. "I like talking to you after I'm done working. I like hearing about your theories and your studies. I like talking about the psychology behind my kinkery and why I like to tie people up.

Did I tell you that when I played soldiers as a kid, I always got the most satisfaction when I tied my action figures up?"

"Yes, you did tell me that."

Owen's fingers found the elastic of my panties. Instead of moving the fabric to the side, he traced it along the length of my abdomen.

"That means my problems likely stem from adolescence, right?" he said. "It's my parents' fault that I'm this way?"

"There's nothing wrong with you, Owen."

"No?" He ran his fingertip just beneath the elastic of my panties. "Even though I like a woman to be helpless and immobile when I fuck her?"

"A lot of women fantasize about being forced into submission."

"Like you?"

I shrugged, even though the blanket and his hold on me made it difficult to effect the movement. "Most of my girlfriends are this way. Women who are in roles of power and want to feel someone more powerful than them take the reins in the bedroom, even if for a short time."

"If he can only last a short time," Owen said as he slid his index finger down into the seam of my core, "then he's not that powerful."

I'd thought my body was sated from the attention they'd given me before. I was wrong. I arched into his touch. Unlike his brother, who would've withdrawn his finger, Owen went right for my clit.

"Your desires aren't anything to be ashamed of," I told him as he made light circles around my bud. "That's what my work is about: erasing the shame from kink."

"You're going to make a great sex doctor."

"Hmmm," I moaned as his index finger made the circles tighter and tighter. "If I can pass my defense."

And that's when it hit me. What had taken place in this room. There had been four people in this room not too long ago. Me, the twins, and Professor Sinead. I'd had an orgasm in front of my dissertation chair.

I closed my eyes and groaned, but not in the good way, despite what Owen was doing to me. "I can't believe I nutted in front of my teacher."

"That's nothing to be ashamed about." Owen stroked my hair with his free hand. "I've fucked a lot of teachers."

How was I going to face Professor Sinead on Monday? Well, at least I'd proven my point about qualitative methodology.

Wait? Had I? The last thing I remember was

Professor Sinead telling me I still needed a quantitative section. Something or other about frequencies.

The thinking section of my brain was fried with Owen making those perfect circles around my clit.

"You're tense, Kellie. Do you want another orgasm?"

I opened my mouth to protest. I wasn't usually this greedy. That was because I was usually buried in my research. But what the hell?

With the hand that wasn't under the covers, Owen pulled the blanket tight around me until I couldn't move. Just around my upper body. My legs were still splayed open in his lap. His thumb and index finger were now working in tandem as he drove me higher and higher.

"Hey, Kellie?" Owen said, his lips hovering over mine. "Do you mind if I kiss you?"

"I..." Did I? Looking at Owen's crooked smile, I knew I wanted to taste his lips. "Sure."

That crooked grin widened as he came closer, closer. Then his mouth was on me. Owen's lips were soft and hot, sweet and spicy.

He matched the thrust of his tongue to the thrust of his index and middle fingers, which pumped inside me. His thumb kept those tight circles going round and round my clit. The orgasm slammed into me before I had time to realize it was close.

"Crushed that level," he said, right before he captured my orgasm with his lips. "How's that dopamine, Dr. Prince?"

I couldn't answer. I couldn't move, either, with the blanket holding me tight. Plus, there was also the case of Owen's fingers still pinging my controls.

He crooked his fingers inside me and pulled another orgasm out. I lost count of the frequency and the ratio schedule. By the time he was done, all my natural chemicals were again out of whack.

CHAPTER NINE

"Do you want me to take care of you?" I asked this as Owen lay back in the corner of the couch.

His legs were splayed in a wide man spread. There was a very impressive erection bulged to the right of his pants. He had one hand curled behind his head, and the other was at his mouth, where he licked the juices he'd gathered from between my legs.

I stood over him, straightening my clothes and trying to put myself back to rights after he'd pulled three toe-curling orgasms from me with just his fingers.

"No, I'm good," he said after a long lick of his middle finger. "When I introduce you to my dick, I want it in that sweet, wet pussy of yours. Not in your hands. Not in your mouth."

This he said while putting his fingers into his mouth again for another long suckle. Then he flicked his tongue at the webbing between his fingers. Owen had fingered me deep. I knew my juices were all over his knuckles and down into his palm. Even though I'd had four orgasms in this room tonight, my body was raring to go for a fifth.

"But I can't have that until you finish your assignment," Owen was saying. "That's the deal."

Fuck, why had I made that deal? It had been a long time since I'd had a good fuck. And with what Owen was packing, I knew it would be a phenomenal fuck.

"Hey, my eyes are up here." Owen grinned and shifted his hips.

I grabbed a pillow from the corner of the couch and threw it at him. He chuckled as he caught it.

"Go be a good girl and ace your assignment so I can fuck you senseless next week, okay, Dr. Prince?"

Oh, he was a smart one, all right. Dangling his carrot of a dick while engaging my need for praise as well as my competitive streak. Now not only were my endorphin levels off the chart, but the adrenaline had kicked in. I was off balance internally. But I somehow felt balanced enough to stand on my own two feet and walk out of the room.

Okay, I might have wobbled a bit. What girl wouldn't after reaching her highest level of orgasms scored in an hour? Owen planted a light kiss on my cheek and sent me off with a "See you after you pass your final, Dr. Prince."

I wobbled again as I walked out the door. I just had to make sure that I did pass. And to do that, I'd have to do some math. Ugh.

I walked out of the room without another word, intent on getting back to my dissertation. Before I could leave the club, Owen's reflection caught my gaze. But Owen never smirked. I had never kissed that cruel mouth.

I wondered if Alan's kisses would be punishing and demanding like he was. The gleam in his eyes dared me to come over and find out for myself.

"Don't drip on the floor, Kellie. I just cleaned up," Alan said as he wound the last bit of rope around his arm. He bent over and placed the rope in a duffle bag, along with his cleaning supplies.

I stood staring at the belly of the bag, trying to remember exactly how to walk away. Something or other about putting one foot in front of the other.

The problem was neither of my legs wanted to be the first to move away from him.

"You realize that professor of yours wants to fuck you," said Alan as he swaggered toward me.

Just like my legs wouldn't move, neither of my lips wanted to part to take on that particular statement. Or maybe they wouldn't move because Alan's gaze was locked in on my mouth. It felt like if I made any sudden moves, he'd be on me.

"It's because you're a student that he hasn't already fucked you, am I right?"

"I don't know what Professor Sinead wants other than me to be a math wiz."

"I thought you were a wiz, Kellie. I thought you were the smartest girl in the class."

Alan was standing so close to me that I could smell the vanilla on his lips. His brother smelled of chocolate and he of vanilla. It was a heady combination. It was scrambling my brains.

And he was complimenting me. That always made me squirm in the good way.

"Why don't you do what he wants?" Alan said. "You're usually such a good girl."

"Am not." Why did he always turn me into a brat? I was a strong, confident woman. But damn if I didn't want this man to take me over his knee.

"I think he's right, though," I admitted. "I think I do need to have a quantitative portion to my work. The asshole."

"You know what I think?" Alan reached for one of my locks. He twined it around his index finger in a mirror motion of what his brother had done to me just moments ago. "I think you're stalling for my dick."

"Puh-lease," I huffed. "I'm saving you from my bomb-ass pussy because it'll ruin you for others."

"That's very thoughtful of you, Kellie."

"You're welcome. I'm a thoughtful kinda girl."

Alan rubbed his thumb against my coiled hair until the blood drained from his index finger. He was standing close enough to kiss me. Unlike his brother, he didn't lean in.

"Why don't you just fuck me now?" I asked. "Clearly you want to."

"You do realize edging is my kink."

Yeah, I did realize that. Alan liked to push his play partners to the edge of pleasure, bring them back, and push them to the edge again. When I'd told him that he'd have to wait until after I graduated to have me, it engaged his kink. Of course it did. It wasn't my first day at this rodeo.

"And once I finish my paper," I said, "and you fuck me, that'll be all."

Having the Carson twins was always going to be my graduation gift to myself. A one-time-only gift. Definitely one for the books.

Alan allowed my tendril of hair to unravel from his finger. "Probably not."

I perked up at that.

"My brother's in love with you, so he'll likely pursue you until he has that bomb-ass pussy on lockdown."

I looked back to the room where I'd left Owen. It should freak me out that he wanted more. I hadn't had a boyfriend... well, I'd never actually had a boyfriend. A string of lovers. But I'd never been monogamous.

Could I be?

Did I want to be?

The thought of Owen Carson and that lovely bulge in his pants just a finger crook away was an enticing thought. It left me feeling warm and secure. Just like when he'd tie me up tight or wrap me up in a blanket and make me come. A girl could get used to that.

I turned back to Alan. "But not you?" I asked.

"Nope, I just want to fuck you." There was a tick

in his jaw as he said the words. "My brother and I have been sharing since the womb. If you're with him, he'll let me play with you. And by play, I mean I'll edge you so far that you will see stars when I finally let you come."

I snorted and then turned on my heel. I had to put some distance between us before I took him up on that offer. "You'll want me so bad, your dick will be weeping before you're even halfway inside me."

"Finish your paper and we'll see who comes first."

Right. My paper. That put a damper on things. It also put another wobble in what would've been an epic strut as I walked out the door. Damn Professor Sinead and his quantitative demands.

CHAPTER TEN

I went home with the intention of taking a cold shower after my night with Professor Sin and the Carson twins. However, it soon became apparent that standing in the porcelain under a spray of ice-cold droplets wouldn't be necessary. The very thought of wrangling statistics cooled my ardor faster than I could reach for the cold knob over the tub basin.

Instead, I slipped into a pair of rainbow-colored sweats with a unicorn on the butt. I dug deep in my hall closet, where I'd stored all the notes from classes over the years. I had to reach way, way, way in the back before I came to my old notes from Professor Sinead's Quantitative Methodology in Behavioral Sciences class.

I'd written most of those notes in black ink. It was rare for me to write anything in black ink. All of my notebooks were an array of the rainbow with notes and my thoughts on the lecture color coordinated by day of the week, section from the text as opposed to the lecture from the professor. But I hadn't understood anything in that class. Not from the text or the teacher or the online YouTube videos where some young math geek tried to make the math fun and failed miserably. Hence the black ink.

It was the first time I'd faked my way through anything, be it in the bedroom or in the classroom. And he knew. Professor Sinead knew that I hadn't grasped the concepts he was trying to explain. I could tell he knew by the snide comments he left on my papers and worksheets.

Were you even paying attention during my lecture, Ms. Prince?

Did you read the assigned material, Ms. Prince?

You're better than this, Ms. Prince.

He was wrong. I wasn't better than this. Even after listening to him instead of staring at him during his lectures, even after reading each chapter twice, sometimes three times, the material just made very little sense to me.

I'd had no issues with math in school. It was

when math was correlated to people and their emotions or actions that I became lost. I had never believed that human beings could be reduced to numbers. There were too many shades of gray.

Unfortunately, it looked like I would have to do that if I wanted to pass this class. If I wanted to successfully defend my dissertation. If I wanted to get fucked in the way I needed to by the Carson twins.

I slid my old notes away from me. For the first time since that stupid quantitative class, I felt like I was spinning. During Professor Sinead's class was when I came back to the scene on a more regular basis. I'd get so riled up fussing with numbers that I needed to be tied up later that night in order to regain my focus and equilibrium for the next day.

My hand hovered over my cell phone. The pull to call Owen was so strong. I knew he could make me relax, maybe even help me see my way through this data set just by tying me up in tight little knots.

As soon as I thought it, I knew my thinking was wrong. Owen wasn't the man I needed. So I pulled my big girl panties on. And by big girl panties, I mean I pulled on a lace black thong under a short skirt and headed out.

I pulled up to the campus early the next morning. Professor Sinead was an early riser. He liked to get in to class at least two hours before his first lecture. I knew that because I had often passed him on my way out from a late night studying in the library.

Sure enough, the man himself was behind his desk taking a sip of his coffee when I darkened his doorstep. If he was surprised to see me, he didn't show it.

"You were... right," I said.

"Come again?"

The blush swarmed my cheeks before my brain could process his words. Was I mistaken, or did the corner of Professor Sinead's eye twitch at his choice of words?

"I'm trying to include a quantitative data set, like you said, but I'm stuck," I said as I marched into the room. I slammed my black and white notes and colorful pens and calculator down on his desk. "I was almost finished. It was perfect until you showed up and showed me my flaw. Now I can't get it out of my head."

"I knew you wouldn't be able to." Professor Sinead leaned back in his chair. He brought his right hand up to rub at his chin as he did so. The flex of his biceps made my mouth water.

"You bastard," I hissed.

Professor Sinead cocked his head and raised his eyebrow, an indication that I'd gone too far. He was right. I was completely far gone.

"I've tried to map the central tendencies," I said. "But the values are all askew."

He nodded at me patiently. "The central tendencies would show you the mean, median, and mode. That's not what you're looking for at this juncture."

"I don't know what I'm looking for."

"Of course you do, Ms. Prince. You are one of the most brilliant minds I've come across in these walls."

"I am?"

Professor Sinead lowered his eyebrow. He looked away from me, but it was too late. The praise was out there. "You know you are. And I know you're smart enough to figure this out."

I arched my back. If anyone had asked, I would've said it was to remove my backpack. My backpack sat at the entrance to the classroom, so that was a lie. I arched my back because I wanted this man to run his hand over me to find the mean, median, and mode of all of my curves.

"Maybe I should start with a dispersion measurement," I said as my nipples hardened with the thought of his fingers dispersing to cup my mounds.

Professor Sinead's glance dipped down to my twin peaks, but he didn't reach out. "No."

I was more disappointed that he was saying no to my answer to his question than my sexual advance. My back caved in and breasts dropped as I slumped down, my hands going onto his desk.

"You're guessing, Ms. Prince. I need you to think." His index finger came under my chin to tilt my head up. "Try again."

It was the first time that he'd ever touched me. I stared into those eyes. I could see him pulling for me. I wanted to please him.

I told my brain to think. "I'm looking for the frequency of occurrences."

"Yes."

"So I should first turn each occurrence in a data set into a percentile value."

"And what might that tell you?"

I watched his lips form the words, and then my brain kicked into gear. "It should tell me the standard deviation of kinkery across all my subjects."

A slow grin spread across his face. "Good girl."

A tendril of my hair slid forward between us. It brushed against the side of the finger that still held my chin up. Professor Sinead's gaze went to that single lock of hair.

Slowly, gently, he pulled the lock toward him. I held my breath, hoping against hope that he would… and then he did. He wound the lock of my hair once, twice around his index finger.

That was all the foreplay I could stand.

I leaned in and brushed my lips against his. Professor Sinead gasped and pulled back. Not out of my reach. Just enough to break the kiss.

He still held my hair coiled around his finger as he stared at me. I saw the battle in his eyes. That bright flick of desire along with the cool assessment that I was so used to. In the next breath, the fire flared and burned all logical thought from his vision, and his lips crashed into mine.

Professor Sinead gave a tug of my hair, and I came to him. My papers fell to the floor as he plunged into my mouth. My legs spread as he pulled my thighs closer to him from his seated position.

My bare ass met the warm wood of his desk and the hot flesh of his fingers. My sneakers squeaked as they came to rest on the sides of his rolling chair. Or maybe that was Professor Sinead shifting his ass in his tailored suit to get closer to me.

I met him more than halfway, tugging at his tie, winding it around my wrist to get a deeper taste of him. It wasn't until the sound of footsteps and voices in the distance registered that we both pulled away.

CHAPTER ELEVEN

My thighs pressed together from the stickiness between them as I bent down and picked up my notes. Professor Sinead was slow to move from his seated position. He took a few extra seconds to rearrange his tie and button his suit jacket before standing to greet the man at the door.

"Another disagreement with one of your students, Chase?"

From my vantage point close to the ground, I spied the big disagreement that I'd just had with Professor Sinead. That little problem was too big for his suit jacket to hide. Hell, the thing rested snug against his thigh, hanging more like a tie than a normal cock. My mouth watered, and I couldn't be sure a droplet didn't splatter onto the black and white notes, turning the markings into a shade of gray.

"You always seem to get the passionate students," said the man in the doorway.

It was Dr. Bryce Santos. The man was a few years older than Professor Sinead. There was gray at his temples, but the streaks were so symmetrical that I wondered if they weren't the product of a high-priced salon to make him look wise. I wouldn't put it past Dr. Santos.

I had never had the man as a teacher. All of his courses were in advanced statistics. Those were elective classes, and few here at the university elected to take them. It was surprising the man was still employed at the university with such low class sizes.

"Ms. Prince solved a statistical problem and became excited at her newfound understanding."

It amazed me that Professor Sinead could say that with a straight face. With a straight, strained face. My gaze dipped to his lips. How could Dr. Santos not see that his colleague's lips were swollen from kissing? How could he not feel the heat of the desire that he'd just walked in on?

I was the most scantily dressed of the three of us,

and there was definitely sweat on my brow. My boobs were still on high alert. And I swear there was a trickle of desire running from my core down my upper thigh. If anyone was going to give anything away, it would be me. I had to get out of there and get myself together.

"Thank you for your help, Professor Sinead. I'll be out of your way now." I gathered my notes into one hand and prepared to rise.

"Stay," commanded Professor Sinead.

And just like the little slut submissive that was inside me, I held still. I was still in a crouch, my body bent in prostration. My knees knocked together as though wondering why they weren't on the floor like a good little sub. The rest of my body had gotten the memo.

My head bowed. My shoulders went back. My hands opened, palms up, and let the note pages slide back to the floor. All of me held still in supplication, hoping to get another taste of him. From this vantage point, I could still see that the ardor between his thighs hadn't cooled. Even with the fabric covering it, I saw that the thickness sat unmoved against Professor Sinead's upper thigh.

"I hear you're up for the position of department

chair," said Dr. Santos, effectively ignoring me. "I just wanted to come and congratulate you."

"Thank you, Bryce. It's the next logical step in my career. I hear you've put your hat in the ring as well."

"That is correct." The two men eyed one another with faux friendly half-smiles. "Well, may the best man win."

Professor Sinead inclined his head slightly, the half-smile neither retreating nor advancing.

Dr. Santos turned on his heel and walked with steady steps to the door. With another glance over his shoulder, he lowered his brow, taking me in again. That's when I knew he didn't stand a chance. Not when he couldn't so much as manage a brow raise.

It was then that I remembered that I was still crouching on the ground. I realized the absurdity of my stance and brought myself to standing. The door snicked closed, and Professor Sinead and I were alone.

The air was still charged between us. There was silence outside. His classes weren't starting for another twenty minutes. That was enough time to at least pull his pants down, slip my panties to the side, and finish what we'd started.

I stared at the closed door. It was never closed.

That was his rule. Professor Sinead took the open-door policy to an extreme, and I understood why.

"You're up for a promotion?" I asked.

"Hmmm," was his response.

"I guess that makes sense. Though logically, I would've thought the next step for a man of your skill in behavioral sciences would be to work in the field, not in the classroom. You could help thousands of regular people a year instead of just a couple dozen students."

Professor Sinead's jaw twisted as he regarded me. I wasn't sure if it was because I challenged his future, or if it was because of what just happened in the not-so-distant past.

"That can not happen again," he said.

"I know," I said, taking a step toward him. "It was pretty close."

"No." Professor Sinead put up his hand. His forearm was pushed straight out as though he would strongarm me if I came near him. In fact, he took a step back away from me and toward the door.

I only knew a handful of people whose safe word was *no*. My friend Josie was one of them. She believed if her body told her no, then that was the end of the scene. She didn't want to have her brain, or her play partner, trying to interpret any other word for stop.

While my brain heard Professor Sinead loud and clear, my body was so used to words like pineapple, Beetlejuice, and Justin Bieber to call the end to fun. With those words in mind, I took another step forward.

"That's enough, Ms. Prince."

Wait? Was he actually saying no to me?

"You're a student," he said. "There's a no fraternization policy. I could lose my job."

"I won't be a student after my defense."

"If you are successful in surpassing your defense."

My brain was a bit scrambled trying to substitute the word no for its actual meaning. Was I now adding prefixes to words that didn't need them? I only had to pass my defense, not *sur*pass it.

"The paper you turned in to me last week would've passed," said Professor Sinead as he opened the door to his classroom. "I don't expect you to only pass. Like I said, you have one of the most brilliant minds that I've ever had the pleasure of teaching. I expect great things out of you."

I may have spontaneously orgasmed standing in front of him. That was more praise than I could handle. The endorphins flooded my veins and made me feel like I could fly.

"Fix your data set," said Professor Sinead.

"When I fix my data set and kill it at my defense, then you'll fu… analyze my measurement tool?"

Professor Sinead's nostrils flared. His lips parted, and he tugged his lower lip into his mouth. I got a peek of his pink tongue. The sight of it reminded me of how it felt plunging into my mouth.

Unbidden, I took a step toward him.

Professor Sinead let out a long, low sigh. His gaze never left mine. Just the heat coming off him was enough to give me a good suntan.

"What would your kink meter tell you, Ms. Prince?"

"I don't need the meter—"

"Yes, you do. Solve the equation and then you'll have the answer you want."

Did he just cock block me with math? "Bastard."

A slow grin spread across Professor Sinead's face. He took one, then two steps forward. His stride was so long that that was all it took for him to stand before me. He dipped his head and brushed his lips against mine. Just a taste. And then he moved to the side and out of my reach.

"I expect exceptionalism, Ms. Prince. Do not disappoint me."

I wouldn't. I was gonna solve the hell out of this equation. And then I was going to rock Professor Sinead's statistical world.

CHAPTER TWELVE

I hate math.

Like, hate it. Like, if it was a cockroach on the wall, I'd spray it with Raid. Then stomp it. Then burn it.

But like the cockroach that math is, the little fucker would probably survive the poison-stomp-fire and crawl back on my wall the next night. Because here it was the next night after Professor Sin left me all hot and bothered and unsatisfied, and I still couldn't quantify this formula to figure out my data set.

I was running out of time. My dissertation defense was in just three days. If I didn't solve this data set, incorporate it into the main body of my work, and do one last read-through, I was fucked. And not in the way I wanted to be.

I was tired. My body ached. My brain was foggy. I was so irritable that both Maree and Josie begged off girl's night and told me to go get a massage instead. Or better yet, get laid.

They were right on that front. I needed a release. But I'd missed my last session at the club with the twins because I was drowning in dispersions and decimals and percentiles. I was fucked, so I didn't have time to get fucked.

Though now I was regretting not keeping my appointment with the boys. With my stress level through the roof like this, I knew the only way to unwind would be to get wound up. If I didn't get the release that being bound and suspended would give me, I wouldn't be able to think clearly to solve my problems, and I would fall flat on my ass.

The spinning in my head was making my ears ring. The ringing got so loud that I grabbed for a pillow and shoved it over my face. Only that didn't shut up the bell tone.

Because it wasn't in my head. It was the doorbell.

It was likely Maree and Josie coming to check on me. Even though they banned me from happy hour, they would never abandon me totally. They were used to this kind of behavior from me, especially in the early days of my thesis. I'd get so focused on my academic work that I didn't take time out for self-care—namely going to the club and getting a little knottical release.

They were going to bitch when I told them I didn't have time to come out and play with them. I had to get this shit done or I wouldn't be able to play at all. Not in my future career, but also not with the Carson twins. And even worse, not with Professor Sin.

I opened the door, preparing to let my girls down. Neither Maree nor Josie were standing on my doorstep.

"Hey, beautiful."

"Owen?"

Sure enough, Owen Carson brightened my welcome mat. A blond curl fell over one bright blue eye. He swiped it back, his lips tugging into a wide grin. The blue of his gaze sparkled at me. He was sunshine even though it was the dead of night.

"What are you doing here?" I asked.

"You missed your scene with us," he said as he walked past me and into my apartment, not bothering to wait for permission.

"And so you stalk me and track me down?"

"Stalk?" he said as he looked around my place.

It looked like a kid had thrown a temper tantrum at an office supply store in here. There were sheets of paper on every surface. Some inside colorful folders. Other pieces crumpled into tight wads. Pens were aimed in every direction, like a circle firing squad.

And then there was me, standing at the center of it all, looking like a defeated general. My face was free of makeup, my hair knotted up on my head in a toppling bun. I couldn't remember the last time I'd washed my face or brushed my teeth.

Even with my apartment and my person in disarray, I still had some of my wits about me. "Yes, stalk. I never told you where I lived."

"No, you didn't," said Owen. "Your friends did."

I had trouble believing that. Maree was always the one to make sure I snapped a photo of any guy I played with. Josie would cyber stalk all the guys I saw more than once.

"And they said if you turned up with a hair out of place that they would cut off my dick and stick it up my ass."

Now that sounded like my girls. "That still doesn't explain what you're doing here in my apartment."

"Like I said, *you* missed your scene with us, which means that *I* missed my aftercare."

There was a part of me that softened at those words. Owen had said he liked playing with me at the end of his night so that he could chat and cuddle with me. That was his way of winding down after a night of play. I wanted to give that to him. I wanted to do that for him. But the part of me that was too busy to play and insisted I get back to work was too loud in my head.

"I'm sorry, Owen. I don't have time. I have to finish my dissertation."

"That's the other reason I'm here. Your friends think you need a break."

"I can't—"

"Come here."

Owen held out his hand. In it was a piece of rope. Like a Pavlovian dog, my trigger was pulled, and I did as I was told to get the reward I so desperately wanted. I came to Owen and offered him my hands.

"You look like you need it as much as I do," said Owen.

He was right; I did. Looking closely at Owen, I saw the same tiredness in his eyes that I felt. We both were experiencing a bit of sub drop—me more acutely than him.

I expected Owen to tie me up and strip me down. He did bind my wrists, but he left my clothes on. He led me to the chair at my desk and sat me down. Strong hands came to my shoulders and began to knead. The groan I let out sounded positively orgasmic.

"That's better, isn't it?"

It was better than better. It was brilliant. Under Owen's magical hands, my body loosened up one vertebra at a time. With my body relaxing, my brain fog began to clear.

"Does your brother know you're here?" I asked.

"Al dropped me off."

"But he didn't come in?"

Owen found another kink in my shoulder blades and rubbed until it gave way. I was melting into a puddle, and so I forgot my question until he answered a moment later.

"Alan's not good with the emotional stuff. He just wants to fuck you. And we can't do that until you pass your class. Right?"

"Right."

Owen's touch gentled as his thumbs made his way down my spine. The gentle kneading of him pressing into me with his left and then his right thumb was hypnotic. I wanted to reach behind and pull him to me to taste his lips. But I couldn't. He'd bound my hands to keep me still.

"Owen?"

"Hmm?"

"Alan said he thinks you're falling in love with me."

"Yeah."

"Wait—Yeah as in yes? Or yeah, as in...?"

"Yeah."

I swallowed a few times, but it was hard for me to digest that nugget of information. "I don't see how that's possible. You barely know me."

"You're smart. You're beautiful. I like talking to you." Owen's hands had traversed the entire route of my spine. His hands were now on my hips, his thumbs rubbing circles around the outline of my sacrum.

"That's it?" I asked. "That's all?"

"Should there be more to it than that?"

"It's only three data points. Can you fall in love with someone with only three data points?" I twisted my upper body to try to see his face.

"You're the scientist, you tell me."

It couldn't be enough. There had to be more to it than that. And besides the quantity, it was qualitatively crazy.

Love needed time. It needed context. It needed more data points. Right?

But here was Owen who said he loved me in such a short time with little data. Then there was Professor Sinead, who had known me for years and had lots of data on me, but he was fighting feelings that were clearly there. And then there was Alan sitting in the middle. He'd had enough data and time to know he wanted to fuck me, but not enough to proclaim any emotional feelings.

"Wait, that's it," I said.

"That's what?"

"I figured it out. I know how to fix my dissertation!" I raised my hands to reach for a pen at my desk, but I ran into a bit of a problem. "Um, can you untie me so I can get to work?"

CHAPTER THIRTEEN

"In my research, I aimed to explore the lived experiences of individuals involved in the BDSM culture. My purpose was to determine how they perceived their level of kink or sexual deviancy."

There was a butt squidge in the otherwise quiet room. My gaze immediately tracked to Professor Sinead. He sat immobile, his forearms braced on the chair and his gaze intent on me.

It had to come from someone else in the room. Perhaps it was stuffy Dr. Santos. He kept checking his expensive watch like he had somewhere else to be. Or maybe it had come from Dr. Wroth. But no. She sat back in her chair far too regally to fidget.

It was clear that neither of them was impressed

with my topic of study. Though I wouldn't peg either of them for the plain vanilla variety. Dr. Santos's pinched expression as I spoke made me certain that he would be into degradation kink. I bet he was the type to wear a diaper and want someone to wipe his ass.

The regality of Dr. Wroth told me that she would've made a superb Dominatrix in another life. It was clear I had her full attention, but she didn't deign to raise those gray eyes at me more than once.

So no. Neither of those two could've been the butt squidger. It likely didn't come from Sinead. It couldn't be the nervous kind of fidget because I was rocking my defense. So it had to be the anticipatory kind.

I was sure of it when I presented my quantified findings using three data points to show the efficaciousness of my kink meter. The man's lips quirked. It was almost a smile. That's when I knew I'd done it. I'd passed Professor Sinead's final test with flying colors.

His butt must be doing a happy dance in that fitted suit because he knew he was going to have me right after this. Hopefully, he was kinky enough to want to do it in his office, right on his desk. A bed would be overrated with that man, and I couldn't wait for the drive to get to either one of our bedrooms.

"Traditionally, researchers such as psychologists and behavioral specialists have looked at the BDSM culture through external measures." I continued multitasking, giving a flawless presentation while making a sexual plan of attack on my teacher. "I went with a more internalized approach and studied first-hand accounts using sexual praxis that—"

"First-hand?" asked Dr. Santos. There was a twitch to his mouth.

"Yes, sir. I went to a local BDSM club, interviewed participants, and—"

"You watched as they had sex?" asked Dr. Santos.

"That is correct."

I waited in silence as the man let out a long, drawn-out sigh. He looked to his colleagues. Dr. Wroth kept her glance down on the document I'd passed out to each of them. Professor Sinead met his gaze.

"I believe there is much precedence for this form of study," said Sinead. "Specifically the work of Masters and Johnson in our understanding of human sexual response, dysfunction and disorders. Please continue, Ms. Prince."

I could have kissed him for defending my work. I

would kiss him. Just as soon as I finished my defense.

"In reviewing my findings, I was able to determine three data points that allowed me to set a scale for the level of sexual deviancy. Since normal sexual behaviors have been labeled by the flavor of vanilla ice cream, I chose to keep that tradition going on my scale. Vanilla is no longer simply the missionary position of sexual intercourse since people are far kinkier today than even five years ago. Neapolitan is for those who mix a little strawberry fun and dark chocolate into their sex lives. And then, the extreme version is what I like to call the Kitchen Sink flavor."

There was a snort, followed by a cough. I knew the snort came from Sinead. I felt profoundly proud that I'd gotten a rise out of the man.

It had been Dr. Santos who had coughed. "I can't see what this unusual, and damn near pornographic study, will add to the world of serious academia."

Professor Sinead opened his mouth, but then pinched his lips closed. That was fine. I didn't need a man to come and rescue me. I was capable of defending myself, fuck you very much.

"My findings apply to counseling, sexual health, and sexual education. It shows a path to delve deeper into human behavior and psyche. These people who play in BDSM culture are transforming trauma—sexual trauma, emotional trauma, even cultural trauma—and redefining themselves. They're healing others and helping people grow past what has pushed them down both inside and outside of the bedroom."

The room was silent after my impassioned speech. Dr. Wroth's gaze flicked to me. It was a quick flash of understanding. Then she dropped her gaze once more. When she did, I saw deep bags under her eyes. She looked a bit pale and thinner than she should look. But in that flash, when she had glanced up at me, I'd seen a spark of something.

Desire, maybe? Hope, perhaps? I wasn't sure, and she wouldn't look at me again. When she spoke, her voice was soft. I had to lean in to make sure I caught her words.

"It looks like you've completed all the steps of your dissertation," said Dr. Wroth. "You've had high marks from all of your professors, even Sinead."

Dr. Santos glared at Dr. Wroth. She wasn't looking at him to notice. Her gaze was once again on the documents in front of her. Dr. Santos turned his glare to Professor Sinead. That staring contest didn't last long. Professor Sinead glared right back. It was Santos who blinked first.

"Lived experiences are widely regarded as the bargain basement form of data in academic studies, especially when they're anonymously given."

I opened my mouth to lay into this man, but a raised brow from Sinead had me biting my tongue.

"Though I still am unconvinced that this paper and its findings do anything for actual sociology," said Dr. Santos, "it's clear that you have met every requirement to pass."

The taste of blood in my mouth from biting down so hard had me ready to rip this man a new one. A glance from Sinead made me pause. He was smiling. An actual, honest-to-God smile stretched his lips, making him look devastating.

That's when I realized it. It was over. I had passed.

I was standing in the moment where I had achieved everything I wanted. I could now move forward with my future plans. And most importantly, in this moment at least, I was going to get laid by my hot professor.

"Congratulations, Dr. Prince. You have successfully defended your dissertation."

This was it. That was me. I was Dr. Prince. The degree was just a bit of paperwork, but as soon as a

PhD student completed their defense, they were a bonafide doctor.

Dr. Wroth stood, her feet wobbling under her as she did. Professor Sinead reached out a hand to steady her. She shied away from his touch. As she turned to go, I noticed there was what looked like a feather tucked into the bun of her tightly woven hair. She was out the door before I could give it a second glance.

Dr. Santos cleared out as well. He offered no congratulations. Just a sneer directed at me and a glare tossed to Professor Sinead.

The room was now clear, leaving only me and Sinead. I reached for him. But he backed away from my touch.

"Not here," he said.

"Why not? I'm not a student anymore."

"No, but I am still a teacher here. I still have a reputation to protect."

Professor Sinead eyed the closed door. There was no one on the other side. No one coming in.

"So you want to take me back to your place?" I asked.

"I stay in the same building as Dr. Santos." He finally tore his gaze away from the door and glanced down at me. He couldn't quite meet my eye. Just like he couldn't quite meet my gaze after he failed to defend me against Dr. Santos' snide comments the second time. "You have to understand. I'm in line for a promotion. I can't have anything potentially sully that."

"Oh. Oh, I get it. You don't want your reputation sullied by the sex doctor."

"Ms. Prince—"

"It's Dr. Prince," I corrected. "You were going to be calling me God. Now you don't get to call me anything. But as a parting gift, you can watch my ass as I walk out the door."

CHAPTER FOURTEEN

I left the Psy Building, stomping down the steps and nearly taking Chad Hollinger out with my retreat march. I heard the words *bitch* and *slut* tossed at me from behind, but I didn't have the time nor the care to confront that attention-seeker. Besides, I outranked him on even more levels now. He was still a student. I was a doctor.

I tossed my rainbow-colored backpack onto the passenger seat of my car. The carefully collated papers of my dissertation spilled from its guts. The documents slipped out of their binding and flew up like a tornado and then fell down like rain.

Yup, that was pretty much how I was feeling right now. Like my bubble had burst. Like I had gotten to the end of the rainbow and there was no treasure from a well-hung leprechaun. Only rocks and dirt and a storm cloud there.

I'd done it. I'd achieved everything I'd worked for. I was done with my schooling and could now be the teacher myself. I didn't have to answer to anyone any longer.

So why did this victory feel so hollow?

Was it just about Sinead?

I'd never needed anyone to fight my battles for me. But when he'd done so, when he had defended me against that twat Dr. Santos, it had made me feel on top of the world. Like Sinead truly understood and respected me. It had been the best high, the purest air of sub space that I had had a whiff of in years. Now, when he'd taken that support from me, I felt like I'd dropped down to the earth with a splat.

I tugged at my pressed slacks. I wasn't wearing any panties today. I didn't need them because I already knew I was a big girl. I had been anticipating a big boy play date. There were no big boys here. Just ladder-climbing teachers who would leave their student behind at the whiff of a promotion.

Instead of heading home, I headed to the club. It was my happy place, filled with people like me who would understand me. People who wouldn't sneer at another person's sexual proclivities. People who wouldn't rip the ground out from under me… unless I asked them to because I had a shame kink or something.

Like, seriously, how rude are people like that? People like Dr. Santos who would openly try to shame others. Or even Dr. Wroth with her silent condemnation. Society no longer pointed and jeered at the physically or mentally disabled. Not polite society, anyway. So why was it still okay to snort and cringe at what someone did with their clothes off?

Hypocrites.

Sinead was the biggest hypocrite of them all. We were supposed to be naked together right now. But he was keeping his suit and tie on so he could blend in with those prudes. Even though I knew the man was topped off with all manner of deviancy.

I mean, who the hell would watch his student being tied up and made to come while sitting all stoic? Only a Dom would exhibit that kind of behavior. I'd bet he was a Gentle Dom. The type to appear calm, cool, and collected on the outside. But as soon as you push the right button, they become sadistic bastards who delight in meting out punishment.

Yeah, that was totally the vibe I got from him. And now I wasn't going to get vibed by him. I brushed an angry tear from my cheek as I slammed my car door closed and headed for the door of the club.

I felt sorry for Sinead. Really, I did. Because here I was at the kinky carnival. I was about to let my freak flag fly, and I didn't care who saw it.

I burst through the doors of the club, expecting to see naked bodies grinding on the floor. Instead, I had to swat at rainbow-colored streamers hanging from the ceiling. Once I finally managed to get the thin sheets of paper out of my face, I was met with people shouting my name.

What in the name of kinkery was this?

There were banners being held up in the air. Letters of each color of the rainbow proclaimed in some fashion or another, *Congratulations, Dr. Prince.* By the time my brain finally worked out that those colorful words spelled my name, I saw my girl-friends coming toward me, arms open, offering hugs.

Maree swept me up from the right. Josie wrapped her arms around me from the left. The applause and praise grew closer until it surrounded me and swallowed me whole.

Tears stung my eyes. Be it from the swell of praise or the letdown of before, I would never admit to. I eyed the throne being sat down at my feet. It was the Queen's chair. I knew that to be true because a few feathers clung to the upholstery. But the Queen herself was conspicuously absent where the woman was always in the club being paraded around.

I didn't spare the absent regent too much thought. I was seeing double vision. Owen and Alan were at the opposite end of the gauntlet of people who wanted to congratulate me.

For once in his life, Alan couldn't wait. He started toward me, moving through the throng of people who were eager to praise my accomplishments.

"You have helped so many people here in this community," said one such kinkster. "You deserve this for all of your good work in the past and what you will continue to do for all of us."

They were right. This was where I would make a difference. I couldn't help those who didn't want help. Those who wouldn't admit that they needed it.

"Did you bang the professor?" asked Josie. "Was he longer than a ruler?"

"No," I said.

"No, you didn't bang him?" asked Maree. "Or no, he was riding the short bus? Because I highly doubt that with—"

"I'll tell you about it later," I said just as Alan reached me.

He held a thin piece of rope in his palm. It was no thicker than a shoelace. He twined rope through his fingers as he regarded me.

"Is that for me?" I asked.

"No," Alan said, tucking the rope in his back pocket. "I tie people up to give them relief. I fuck as a reward."

Fuck was often the word for affection in this kinky kingdom. Was that what Alan was saying? Did he have affection for me? Did I want him to? Did I feel anything for him?

Alan took my hand and led me away from my party. No one booed at the guest of honor being taken away. Instead, they all cheered. Inside the room Alan led me into, Owen sat cross-legged on the bed. He smiled when he saw me.

"I have a belly ache, Doctor," Owen said, rubbing his six pack.

"I'm not that kinda doctor, Owen."

"You're our kind of doctor," he said. "Take your clothes off so we can see you right now."

CHAPTER FIFTEEN

Neither twin helped me undress. They both sat on the bed and watched my every move, their eyes tracking as if they had one brain. Owen lounged back against the headboard. Alan sat at the edge of the mattress as if sprung to strike at a second's notice.

I kicked off the dress slacks that had been confining me all day. Instead of bothering with buttons, I tugged the blouse over my head. My fingers worked to unfasten the clasp of my bra. Once free, I tossed the scant bit of lace at Alan's face.

"Brat," he said as he caught the lace. He stood then, coming toward me. "Hands."

I felt a bit of relief flood through me as I offered him my hands. I didn't want to be entirely free in this. I wanted them to hold me down. I didn't want many choices. I wanted them to make me do whatever it was that they had planned for me.

Alan, glorious devil that he was, bound my hands with my bra. He even used the metal clasp to secure my hands in place. When he was done, my double-Ds were propped up by nothing but my forearms.

With my upper body properly trussed up, Alan guided me to the bed. He shoved me down onto Owen's lap. Instead of immediately pulling his dick out, Owen held my face between his hands.

"Hey, Kellie," he said against my lips.

"Hey, Owen."

"I missed you today."

Owen traced my lips with his own. He didn't use his tongue. He didn't press his suit. He simply rubbed his mouth against mine, whisper-soft, until I finally moaned with need. That's when he began to kiss me, slowly, leisurely, as if he had all the time in the world.

My hands were being lifted up and over my head from between us. My body was flipped over until I lay on my back with my arms stretched over me and my legs stretched out. Alan attached my bra straps to the headboard of the bed. I got the shock of my life when he took my lips as he lay on the other side of me.

I hadn't expected Alan to kiss me. I hadn't imagined that was his thing. His kiss was nothing like his brother's. Alan's kiss was hungry, like he hadn't eaten in a long time. Come to think of it, I'd never seen him kiss one of his clients, let alone fuck one of them. This was purely for me.

Yeah, I think I was starting to *fuck* him, too.

I heard the crinkle of not one, but two condom wrappers, and my excitement increased. At my back, Owen nudged his thick length inside of me. Just the tip. Just enough to make me squirm against him, begging for more. Oh, so now he wanted to be the tease?

"Owen, please," I begged, arching my back and trying to get my ass more firmly seated on his cock. But he wasn't having it.

Owen hooked one of my legs over his hips. He had the right leverage and the right angle to plunge himself into me fully. Instead, he kept playing with the tip.

I growled in frustration, but it sounded much like my moans of pleasure. Because it felt good. It all felt so good.

Just when I thought I couldn't stand any more,

Alan slid down the bed. He put his face between my thighs and went to work. His tongue traced tight circles on my clit as Owen continued to pump into me. His strokes went gradually deeper and deeper until the orgasm slammed into me and I pulled against my restraints.

It was my clenching muscles that finally pulled Owen all the way inside of me. The strength of my desire might've pulled him, but the man refused to be pushed around. He continued with his own rhythm—slow and deep.

Alan's tongue laved, licking up all the juices from my orgasm. He licked his way back up my body, still taking his time. He played in my belly button as his brother twisted his hips. Owen's thick cock found another pleasure spot deep inside me, bringing me near the edge again.

That's when Alan pulled my thigh over his hips. It dislodged Owen from my core. That's when Owen began knocking at my back door. Oh, was I eager to let him in.

Alan began a light tapping at my front door with his cock. The twins weren't nearly identical in just their faces. I bet their cocks matched, too. They sure as hell did in feel and fit.

I had a real moment of panic, thinking the two

of them together inside of me wouldn't fit. With my hands bound over my head and my legs spread between them, I could do nothing but receive. With two visitors coming at me from opposite ends, I was so dizzy that it stole my breath. I couldn't speak. I'm glad I couldn't because by the time they both made themselves at home inside me, I was so thankful I'd laid out the welcome mat.

"Fuck," Alan whispered as he gazed down at me, his dick fully lodged inside my core.

"Yeah," I said. "Fuck you too."

Alan grinned. That grin told me all I needed to know. There was definite affection there. And it was a two-way street.

"I love you, Kellie," Owen said into the cone of my ear.

Well, that made his feelings crystal clear. I wanted to say it back to him. But I wasn't sure if I meant it. Not in the way he meant it. And I think I wanted to mean it when I said it. Right now, I was in a sex haze.

The boys pumped into me, making me damn near lose consciousness with all the pleasure. Owen came inside of my ass with a guttural yell. He clutched me close to him, whispering those same three words over and over again like he was sending up a prayer.

Once Owen finally released me, Alan slipped beneath me, twisting my arms and my body until I was overtop of him. My arms were still bound, my body stretched.

Alan pumped up and into me, his thrusts long, deep, hard, unyielding until I came again. Alan came right behind me. He didn't yell his release. He sighed it, like he was answering a prayer of his own.

When I finally caught my breath, I could only manage four little words. But I said them with conviction from the bottom of my heart.

"I fuck you both."

CHAPTER SIXTEEN

I walked through the campus quad, eyes straight ahead, one foot in front of the other. I had to do that, otherwise I would be walking crisscrossed. The Carsons had done a number on me last night, and I couldn't wait to get back to them for round three.

At some point, we'd left the club and made it back to my place. The boys had made themselves right at home. Owen had made a late-night breakfast spread for us. I had my belly filled, and then they filled me in an even more pleasurable way.

This morning, Owen had pecked me on the cheek with a casual, "Love you, babe" as I got dressed.

Alan hadn't gotten dressed at all. He'd lain naked,

twisted in my covers. His eyes tracked my every movement as I pulled on colorful leggings and a fitted, white T-shirt. Once I was properly attired, he said, "I'm gonna fuck you senseless when you get back."

If those two sentiments didn't make a girl feel adored and cherished, then I don't know what would.

I quickened my pace as I neared the Psy Building. My goal was to get in and get out. I just needed to deal with a few administrative details now that I'd successfully defended my research.

I didn't care whether I saw Professor Sin or not. Hence the leggings and T-shirt. Even my locks were swept up in a haphazard ponytail that said *I've just been fucked and fucked good and don't you regret that you didn't take your chance and fuck me?* Yup, that's the look I was going for. And I didn't care whether he saw it or not.

I should've asked Owen and Alan to come with me. I would've paraded the twins on my arms so that Sinead could see just how much I didn't care. Because I really didn't care about—

"So you're the one that's going to get Professor Sinead fired."

I turned to that voice. Chad the Douche peeled

away from his lackeys. But not too far away that he wouldn't be heard by them. His voice would've barely registered on my notice, except for the word *fired*.

"What are you talking about?" I said, my foot resting on the first step that would take me up and into the Psy Building.

"Someone reported seeing Sinead screwing a coed, and the administration is now investigating it."

The administration what? Sinead what? What coed? Because it wasn't me. Whoever this *someone* was, they weren't talking about me because that man's dick hadn't gotten screwed into me.

Or maybe they were talking about the two of us. If someone had seen Professor Sinead and me kissing, they could've gotten the wrong idea. I mean, I had tried to get into his pants that day. And we were writhing on each other in a fashion that could've looked like screwing.

"There's been an anonymous complaint," Chad continued, eying me accusingly. Or rather wantonly, like he wasn't so much pissed about the complaint as he was that I hadn't been screwing him.

Whatever. There wasn't a me and him. There wasn't ever going to be a me and him.

And whoever this anonymous complainant was,

it definitely wasn't me. I wasn't the anonymous kinda girl. If I wasn't happy about something, I said it loud and to the person's face. Not behind their back.

I had been wronged in the whole Sinead situation. And I had made my displeasure known to his face. But we hadn't fucked, so there was nothing to complain about. I marched into the building to set it straight.

I stormed into Professor Sinead's office. His back was to me as I came over the threshold. That glorious ass was bent over as he picked something up from a bottom drawer of his desk. His cheeks tensed as he straightened and put it in a box. I was momentarily distracted by his gluteus maximus. But just for a moment.

"What are you doing?" I demanded.

Sinead didn't jerk at the sound of my voice. I'm sure he heard my presence from when I was halfway down the hall. "Use your inductive reasoning, Dr. Prince. I'm packing up my office."

It used to get me off when he called me Ms. Prince. Now that he'd added the Dr. to it, I was ready to spontaneously orgasm. I was a fool to think I was over this man. I was a fool to think I'd ever be over him. I wanted him as much right now as I had the day I'd first walked into his classroom.

He'd been standing tall and proud, his head high in the air like a balloon that was full of knowledge, not air. Right now, his shoulders were hunched as though he was defeated, deflated.

"I didn't take you for the vengeful type," he said.

"What?" I had to run his words through my brain a couple of times. After tearing my gaze away from his ass first. "You think I filed that anonymous report on you?"

He turned now, taking away the sight of his ass and replacing it with the view of his coatless chest. His pecs strained against the white cotton of his shirt. He even had the cuffs of his shirt rolled up to his elbows. *Fuck me*, the man was beautiful.

I took a tentative step toward him. Tentative because I was fairly certain that if I moved too fast, I was going to jump him. "When have I ever not come and said my piece to your face?"

Sinead cocked his head to the side, giving me his thinking face. His thinking face was my second favorite expression. It had been my top fave until I saw what his desire face looked like. Fuck if I didn't want to see that again.

"I said my piece to you that day," I reminded him.

"I didn't go behind your back and try to get you in trouble."

"No, that's not your modus operandi at all. You've never exhibited vengeful behavior. Even with your interest in sexual deviancy, you've always maintained a high sense of morality and honor."

"Thank… you?"

"You didn't do this."

"No, I didn't. It must be some other student you were making eyes at." There was a hidden question mark at the end of that sentence. I looked up at Professor Sinead from beneath hooded lids.

Sinead cocked his head in the other direction, those eyes like lasers on me. I was about to be handed a pop quiz that I had not studied for.

"You don't believe that of me," he said. His question mark hid behind the same wall that mine had.

No, I didn't believe that of him. Just like he knew my character, I knew his.

"You didn't do this," I said with complete certainty.

"Yes. I did. I admitted it."

The wash of cold that ran through my body made my knees buckle. The floor was coming up fast, but I didn't slam down into it. Sinead was there with a hand on my waist to keep me steady. When I still wobbled, he pulled me to him.

"I was inappropriate with one student," he clarified. "I've hungered for her since the moment she sat down in my class. I've imagined doing the filthiest things to her for two years, and I'm not an imaginative man. But fuck, the things I've dreamed of doing to you…"

His gaze was on my lips. Eyes darting from one side of my mouth to the other, then coming to rest on my gaze. I felt like a specimen he was studying. I felt certain I was wearing too many clothes for him to get an adequate picture of me. I had the sudden urge to strip down to my birthday suit.

"I shouldn't have let you walk out the door without…"

"Without what?" I prompted.

"Without me at your side," he said. "I don't give a half a fuck what Santos thinks. And he would've thought some things if I'd gotten you back to my apartment. The walls are pretty thin."

"Oh, fuck," I sighed.

Sinead raised a brow in question. A slow, wicked grin spread across his face. "Would you like a demonstration of the lessons I planned for you, Dr.

Prince? I'll walk out of here with you now like I should've the other day."

"You can't. You have a 2 p.m. class."

Sinead shook his head. "Not anymore. I'm on leave while they investigate my inappropriate behavior with you. Might as well make the most of it."

"They can't fire you."

"They probably will."

"But we didn't fuck. We just kissed. It was consensual, and I didn't file any report."

"It doesn't matter. An accusation like this will ruin my career," Sinead said, pulling me a little closer. I got the sense I was now the anchor he was holding on to.

Sinead dipped his head and kissed me on one side of my mouth. A light kiss that promised wickedness. Then he moved to the other side of my mouth and did the same.

"I can't tell if you kissing me is you giving up. Or you giving in."

"Both," he said before he claimed my entire mouth.

The pop quiz was done. This wasn't a lecture. It wasn't the test. It was the final exam, and damn if I wasn't prepared for what my teacher could do with his tongue. I'd been on the scene for years, but no one had ever tied me in knots with the simple swipe of his tongue.

My knees were buckling again. As they knocked against Sinead's, I felt that his were too. We were trading off being each other's anchor. Which was funny because I, for one, felt like I was sinking. I nearly crashed when I heard a throat being cleared from the open doorway.

"I've seen all I need to see."

That came from Dr. Santos. He stood in the open doorway with the dean of the School of Psychology, Dr. Hernandez. Behind the two dark-haired men, I could just make out the silver-gray hair of Dr. Wroth. While the two men looked on in contempt, Dr. Wroth wore a different expression.

The crow's feet tugged at the older woman's eyes as she stared at us. Her parted lips looked like they were parched. My first instinct was to offer the woman a drink. Her skin looked so pale that I worried she would faint.

"In light of this display," Dr. Santos was saying, "I don't think we need a board review. I move Chase

Sinead be terminated from his position here effective immediately."

"He didn't break the rules," I said, stepping in front of Sinead. "I did. I kissed him when I was a student. He's the one that pushed me away. He's the one that said it was inappropriate because of our teacher-student relationship."

"It didn't look like he was pushing you away now," said Dr. Santos.

"I'm not a student anymore," I said. "So, once again, no rules broken."

Dr. Santos bristled, his chest puffing up like an irate peacock whose feathers were only black and white. Beside him, Dean Hernandez scratched at his salt and pepper chin. Dr. Wroth said nothing, only licked at her parched lips.

What surprised me most was Sinead. For someone who always had all the answers, he wasn't speaking up on his own behalf.

"There's still the complaint," Dr. Santos pointed out.

"An anonymous complaint," I counter pointed. "Where I've given you the facts of what occurred and showed that Sinead did nothing wrong."

"Rules are rules," Dr. Santos went on, but he was speaking to Dean Hernandez, not me. "We still need to investigate the veracity of the complaint."

"That's utter bullshit."

"Watch your language, Ms. Prince."

"It's Dr. Prince. And my two hundred pages of excellent language earned me one of the highest degrees in the world. Yet you're going to take away the career of the most brilliant man here because of unsubstantiated words from an unverified source? Based on what evidence? Someone's word? You mean their lived experience? But I thought lived experiences were widely regarded as the bargain basement form of data in academic studies, especially when they're anonymously given."

Dr. Santos's lips pinched together like a child who was about to throw a temper tantrum. Behind him, I could see a small crowd gathering. Chad's greasy hair was the first person I recognized. He stood to the side of a redhead I vaguely recognized.

"The anonymous report," said Dr. Hernandez, "said Dr. Sinead went to a sex club with a student."

Behind me, I heard Sinead let out a low sigh. It sounded like defeat. Back in front of me, I recognized the only other person who could've put the two of us at the BDSM club together.

"Ginger."

The girl jerked at the sound of her name. Her eyes found mine. There was no love lost in her gaze.

I'd had little to no interaction with her on campus. I'd had only a smidge more interaction with her inside the club. That was mainly impatient foot-tapping when she was taking too long to vacate the platform that the Carson twins used to bind and suspend their clients.

"If you're pissed at me because I'm sleeping with the twins, you don't need to take it out on Sinead."

There was a collective gasp and actual clutching of pearls at that revelation. I heard the word *slut* being bandied about from the peanut gallery. Both Dr. Santos and Dean Hernandez looked at me as though I was yesterday's trash.

It didn't matter what they called me. So long as they added Doctor in front of any slur. I always took responsibility for my actions, and I had no shame in my kink. But I would be damned if I'd let anyone else be used and hurt over my choices.

I took a step forward, ready to bring Ginger to her knees, if that's what it took to get a confession. I liked being on the bottom. When I had a partner or partners who could handle me. But I was a boss bitch Dominant at heart. Ginger didn't stand a chance.

That single step forward I tried to take didn't get me far. Looking over my shoulder, I saw Sinead holding me back.

"It wasn't her," he said.

"How do you know?"

"I know."

Sinead said it as though he was giving a lecture. He said it in that tone that told his students that this question would be on the final exam. He said it like he knew the answer to the question that was posed.

"You know who the anonymous source is?" I asked.

There was a choked sound that came from those gathered outside the door to the classroom. When I looked up, I couldn't tell who it came from. Both Dr. Santos and the dean still wore their expressions of contempt. Chad looked like he was getting off, watching the demise of another person. Ginger looked smug, like she was watching her greatest enemy get their just desserts.

"It doesn't matter," said Sinead. "There's nothing more here that I want to do."

"Now, Chase," said Dean Hernandez, "don't be hasty. I'm sure there's something we can work out."

"You think so?" Sinead asked as he came to stand

beside me. He curled his fingers around mine, giving my hand a tight squeeze that felt like solidarity.

Dean Hernandez took one glance at our entwined hands and pursed his lips. When he glanced back up at Sinead, there was censure in his eyes. "Think about your career. Don't throw it away over a... a..."

"A what?" I asked. "A sex therapist? Or a slut? Doesn't matter to me which one you call me because I'm both."

Sinead chuckled beside me. "She's going to be a brilliant therapist. You should read her study. As for the slut bit, I haven't had a chance to experience that myself. So if you'll excuse us."

Sinead gave my hand a tug. I didn't need much of a pull to follow him. We made our way out of the classroom and into the throng of people. Looking down at the floor, I noticed a feather lying in the spot where Dr. Wroth had once been standing.

CHAPTER EIGHTEEN

"They can't do this to you," I said as I paced the length of my apartment. "I mean, there has to be something we can do. Some higher authority we can appeal to."

"Maple syrup?" asked Owen.

"Yes, thank you," said Sinead.

Sinead offered up his plate of pancakes. There were four, maybe six, of them stacked high. Owen held the comely figure of Mrs. Butterworth syrup and poured a generous amount of the golden brown liquid over Sinead's stack.

"We're not going to take this lying down," I said, coming to stand beside Sinead. "We're going to fight."

"These are seriously fluffy," said Sinead around a mouthful.

"Thanks," said Owen. "It's the buttermilk."

"Really, really good."

"Guys!"

The two men turned to look at me. Owen was dressed in a cooking smock that said *Kiss the Cook*. His chest was bare beneath. His bare feet padded against the linoleum as he turned back to the stovetop to flip another batch of flapjacks.

Sinead was setting on one of my bar stools. He had his shirt on, the cuffs still unbuttoned and rolled up to expose his glorious forearms. His feet were also bare.

It was that sight more than anything that threatened to make me blush: the sight of my former teacher's soon to be lover's bare toes on my kitchen floor. Also, he was giving Owen all the compliments. Here I was trying to solve the mystery of who set him up, and I hadn't gotten a single word of praise yet.

"Focus," I said. "You need to tell me who the anonymous source is."

Sinead shrugged. "It doesn't matter."

"Of course it does. It's your reputation. Someone

is misrepresenting you because of me. I can't let that slide."

"What they said was true." Sinead sliced and dragged a perfect triangle of pancakes through syrup. "I was with a student at a sex club. Technically, two students and..."

"Two students and what?" I asked.

"It doesn't matter. I don't care to go back." To put a period at the end of that statement, he stuffed his mouth full of a ragged cut of pancakes.

"You love your job. You're exceptional at it. I'm not going to let them take that from you."

Sinead set down his silverware. He opened his arms and beckoned me into them. I came willingly. There was a part of me that wanted to drop the argument and get to the fucking, but I couldn't let this go. Not yet.

"I felt restrained in that job," Sinead said once I was in his arms. "For two years, I had to have someone in the classroom or in my office with me at all times to make sure I could never be accused of anything inappropriate. I had to deal with parents of grown adults who wanted to know why their grade was low. I had to deal with idiots who should not have any letters after their names. Not to mention the jealousy and backstabbing of my colleagues."

"If you hated it so much, then why did you stay?"

He looked up at me, his gaze lingering as he sucked at the corner of his thumb where a dollop of syrup stuck to his flesh. Watching his tongue flick over that spot, I became overheated. But not as overheated as I got when I saw the flare of desire in his eyes.

"Me?" I asked. "You stayed because of me."

"And the pay was good." He grinned as he said the words. Chase Sinead grinning was devastating to behold. "The day after your defense, I realized that if you were gone, I really had no reason to stay."

I put my hand on his heart. "I think I fuck you."

"No," Sinead chuckled. "We haven't done that yet."

"You totally should," said Owen. "Her honey is better than that maple syrup."

"Would you tie her up for me, Owen? It's been years since Boy Scouts, and I'm out of practice with knots."

I opened my mouth to protest. I was supposed to be fighting for something. But all I could think about was the feel of the knots restraining me as Sinead breeched my most intimate defenses. Surely there was no need to protest any of that.

CHAPTER NINETEEN

"I don't have enough rope on me to suspend her." Owen stood with his hands on his hips in a pose that reminded me of Superman, except it was a blond lock that hung over his blue eyes instead of jet black. He stared down into the belly of a duffel bag where I saw tan twine snake over the top.

Sinead sat on the bed beside me. He had my legs over his lap and was running his thumb idly over my calf. Just that small touch had me pressing my thighs together. Because I wanted this man inside me in the worst way.

Two years of tormenting teasing was enough. No more pop quizzes. No more tests on the material.

The textbook was out the window, and the live demonstration was about to begin.

"I can tie her legs down and then pin her arms for you," Owen offered.

I swear I came right then and there at just the thought of it.

"I think she would like that." Sinead peered into my eyes as he said it. He was wearing his pensive face, both brows lowered as he stared unblinking into my gaze.

"Oh, I know she would," said Owen. "Get her clothes off, would you?"

I knew that Professor Sinead was an expert in his field. I was now learning the man was an expert at undressing a woman. His fingers were deft as they hooked into my leggings slid the fabric down my legs.

He was efficient, too. Along with the leggings, he managed to capture my lace thong. Sinead stripped both articles of clothing from my body with a single pull. When he paused to gaze down at my bare thighs and exposed core, his throat worked. It was the first time I'd seen the man stumble. I felt both excited and humbled that it was me, my body, that did that to him.

I lifted my arms for him, eager to have my whole

body bare for this man. The cool of his nails was followed by the heat of his finger pads. They brushed my skin as he divested me of both my shirt and my bra. When my head was freed from that last strip of my clothing, I saw Owen's beautiful face smiling at me.

Sinead made my head fill with desire and want. Owen made my chest feel like it was going to burst with joy and, yes, love. There was no question that Owen loved me. It was becoming clearer and clearer that I loved him.

There had been no falling involved. It had just happened. One moment I liked him, the next moment I loved him. With Sinead, I knew there would be a fall involved.

Sinead pushed me down on the mattress. His arm came around my back to cushion the blow. His body came down on top of mine as we crashed down onto the plush mattress together. Any fear about the impending fall I would take with this man was immediately extinguished.

I placed my arms over my head. I opened my thighs to seat him. Inside my body, my heart as well as my core opened, readying to welcome him in.

"Good girl," Sinead said, his lips hovering over mine.

The compliment wasn't enough to placate me. I lifted my head until our lips met. I captured his mouth, licking, sucking, even biting a little.

Sinead allowed it. Meanwhile, Owen tugged my legs to the end of the bed frame. I felt the cool prickle of rope at my ankles as he bound me spread-eagle to the edge of the bed. Once my bottom half was immobile, Sinead took control of the kiss.

His tongue plunged deeply as his fingers worked below to free his erection from his pants. He didn't even spare the time to undress fully. I heard the crinkle of a condom wrapper and then he was inside me.

There was no foreplay. There was no need. I'd been wet for this man for two whole years. His thick cock fairly vibrated as he seated himself fully inside of me, leaving not a centimeter of space in my tight sheath for any give.

With each thrust, he took from me. More and more until I was a ball of need. I needed to get closer to him. I needed to hold on to him. But I couldn't move my hands.

At some point, Owen had come to the head of the bed and claimed my arms. He maneuvered my head into his lap as he stretched my forearms over my head and held me down.

My legs were bound at the bottom. My arms were being held down by the man I loved. All while the man I was falling for plunged into me again and again with punishing thrusts.

I was falling while being held still.

When the first climax crashed over me, I feared I was going to be ripped in two. In a sense, I was. Owen had already claimed a part of me for himself. With his final shuddering thrust, Sinead claimed his piece.

As I slowly regained my breath, and Owen and Sinead traded places, I realized there was a piece of me that was still left dangling. It dangled while my guys gave me a few more orgasms. It swayed as they both wrapped me up in their arms and we all fell into a contented sleep. It nudged me awake when I heard the door to my bedroom creak open and a blond figure darkened the threshold.

"It looks like you're going to need a bigger bed, Kellie."

"Fuck you, Alan." I smiled up at him as I snuggled into his brother's chest.

"Fuck you right back." Alan gave me a wink. Then he turned his nose in the air toward the kitchen. "Do I smell pancakes?"

CHAPTER TWENTY

"So you're dating Professor Sin now?" asked Maree.

I cocked my head to the side. Was this dating that we were doing? Was he my boyfriend? Then what did that make Owen? I knew Owen definitely wanted the label. And even though I was a grown woman, I didn't mind it so much between me and Owen. But it seemed childish to label Chase that way.

"He told me to call him Chase." There was a trill to my voice when I said his name. "Holy fuck, did I just giggle? I do not giggle."

"You just giggled," said Josie. "Having three men worshipping your clit will bring out the giggle even in a grown-ass woman."

I looked over at my three guys. Owen and Alan were prepping ropes for their sessions tonight. There had been a small part of me that chafed that they would still tie up others, but then Alan rubbed a bit of lube between my ass cheeks, and the three of them fucked some sense into me.

As Pro Doms, binding people who wanted the experience of ropes is how they make their living. It's their job, and it has nothing to do with their personal life. I'm the only woman in their personal life. The only person they fuck.

Hell, whenever Owen touched me, it always felt like he was making love to me. And yes, surprisingly, there was a difference. I've felt it. A few times Alan slipped up and a little lovemaking may have rotated his hips one way instead of the other.

Not everyone at the club was happy about this change of relationship status. Many of the women felt they had a chance to end up in the Carson twins' bed. Ginger was one of them. Even though Chase made it plain that she'd complained to him about a low grade, which according to him she did deserve, and wasn't the anonymous tattle teller, she still glared at me when she saw me in the club with the twins.

For his part, Chase wore his perpetual scowl of

disapproval as he watched the twins unbind their last client. The man still had serious resting bitch face. But when he glanced up at me, his features softened a little.

He'd been gone from the university for a week. Slowly and surely, he was loosening up. And by loosening up, he was getting me limber with a lot of sex.

So much sex.

I should be tired. I should be sore. Hell, I should have a UTI.

But nope. My lady bits liked what Chase, Owen, and Alan were doing to me on a nightly, and sometimes morningly, basis so much that I stayed a happy pink and not an angry red.

As for me, I already had a few clients lined up for my new therapy business. A couple were from the club, but I also had a few referrals from some of the Doms who wanted to ensure their subs had the mental healthcare that wasn't so readily available to them by other therapists.

My business was also gaining four walls downtown, and I'd acquired a partner. Chase would be consulting with me there. Not in the sex therapy department. He would deal with the average run of the mill mental and behavioral health issues. Alan and Owen and I were even talking about how they could use ropes and bondage to heal people in therapy.

We were a literal team. I couldn't believe it. I was living in the midst of a real-life happily ever after. Me, the girl who preferred cross-referenced sources to imaginative tales, was living the dream.

"Oh, look," said Maree. "The Queen is back."

Sure enough, the regent was seated on her throne. She wasn't yet thrust up into the air. Her courtiers were at the bar throwing back a drink. But there were a few men eyeing the praise chair as she flung back her gown to reveal her bare bottom. As the dress flitted over the back of the chair, a few of the feathers woven into the gown fluttered to the ground.

Ice crawled down my back as the feathers hit the floor. I glanced back up at the Queen to confirm my suspicions, but before I could take a step toward her, a hand reached out to stop me.

"Leave it, Kellie."

I looked up into Chase's stern gaze. There was a part of me that was programmed to heel at my teacher giving me an instruction. But the part of me that was determining if I wanted to be called his girlfriend or his partner reared.

"No," I said, wrenching my arm out of his hold. "She's going to answer for what she did to you."

I stormed up to the Queen, preparing to unseat her from her throne. She looked up at me. It took only a split second for recognition to dawn before she froze in absolute horror.

"Dr. Wroth."

Queen Wroth looked like she was going to be sick. Her gray eyes filled with tears. Her regal shoulders slumped. She wrapped her arms around herself.

"It was you? You wrote that anonymous letter about Chase, didn't you?"

"I'm sorry. I wasn't thinking clearly."

"You were thinking clearly enough to spell Sinead correctly. Why would you go through all of that trouble to get him fired?"

"I just needed him out of here. This is my place." She lifted her head to look around the club. When she did, a few of the tears spilled from her eyes. "I need this place. I need this club to unwind after the work I do. I couldn't have anyone knowing my secret life."

"But there are students from the university who come here."

Ginger was over in the corner being spanked by

another Dom. I'd seen a few other recognizable faces from the quad in here a time or two. And then there was me, and I was a frequent guest.

"Sinead was a colleague," said Dr. Wroth. "He could get me fired."

"I wouldn't have done that," said Chase from behind me. "Santos or another of our colleagues might have. I've never been one to tear another down."

Chase missed the side-eye I gave him. Or he ignored it. The man had been notorious for ripping students a new one in the lecture hall. Ginger was a case in point.

"Don't you know the first rule of kink club?" I said. "You don't talk about kink club outside of kink club."

"I couldn't risk it, and I couldn't stay away from here much longer. I just needed to get back here."

Dr. Wroth looked unbalanced as she spoke. There was a tremor in her hand. Her eyes, which had been bright and filled with life before she recognized me and Chase, now looked cloudy and weary.

It was clear the woman was in Dom drop. I had heard that the crash that resulted from the loss of endorphins, adrenaline, and oxytocin was more intense for Dominants because of the need for control. Dr. Wroth had been out of the club for at least a week by my count. She must have been at rock bottom before tonight.

"Let me help you," I said, no one more surprised than me that my anger over what she'd done dissipated at the clear signs that she needed help.

Shame colored her face as she met my gaze. I'd never seen anyone look so lost.

"I'll get him his job back if you don't tell anyone about me," Dr. Wroth said.

"No need," said Chase. "I'm happy where I am. My current colleagues don't backstab, unless you ask nicely."

Chase offered Dr. Wroth his hand. After a moment, she took it. He gave a courtly bow of his head. "Enjoy your evening, Laurel. Then come and see Dr. Prince sometime this week. She can help. I'm sure you believe she can after hearing her defense presentation."

Dr. Wroth swallowed, but her head bobbed once in agreement.

Chase took my hand. He twined our fingers together and led me away from the Queen just as her courtiers returned to hoist her into the air. The sounds of her pleasure trailed us as we headed back to the twins.

"Are you sure?" I asked Chase. "About your job, I mean. If she retracts her statement—"

"I meant what I said. I like my new colleagues a lot better than the ones at the university. Besides, the only ladder I'm interested in climbing is the one you're strung up on."

He looked down at me. His lips stretched into that devastating smile.

"Plus, I only want to work with the exceptional," he continued. "And you're the most exceptional person I've ever met in my life."

Chase rubbed his thumb over my lower lip. He had a tough time keeping hold of it because my lips split into the widest, most self-satisfied grin that any woman had ever worn. I should be frightened to feel this happy. If this scene were ever to end, I doubt I would be able to get back on my feet.

But I didn't fear it ending. Not for my whole life. Chase held my hand tightly, like he would never let me go. Then, a second later, his hold loosened.

Chase passed me over to Owen, who held his arms open to me. Owen claimed my mouth for a soul-claiming kiss. By the time he let me up for air, I was breathless.

"There's my girl," he whispered in my ear.

He was right. I was his girl. I was all their girl. And they were my guys.

"You ready to be bound, Kellie?" asked Alan.

I grinned up at him in response. Didn't he know? I was already bound, and these ties would never unravel.

"Yes, I am." I offered Alan my wrists just as I offered them all my heart. "Make me fly."